# Journey into the Soul

I wrote these stories in the 1990's, therefore, the references to songs and other information, relate to that very difficult time in my life.

Only one, 'Tangible Dreams', has been shared with the world. Now that all are available, it is my hope that you enjoy what came out of that dark phase, and possibly find positivity and light in them.

Every human being that has ever lived, or will live, is a soul. Moreover, although, as souls, we have our differences, two things are certain. We all belong to the same race, the human race. And as such, we all experiences the same emotions, love, hate, fear, wonderment, rejection, peace, loneliness, empathy…the list goes on.

In light of these facts, all of us, on some level at least, can relate to the trials which the souls in these stories face, and how they deal with them.

'Journey into the Soul' is about six couples with very different stories. It shows how each couple's lives entwine, sometimes turning everything upside down. When the power of love comes into play, we can overcome seemingly insurmountable obstacles, discover deep human emotions, and come to understand how the heart heals, despite adversities.

Watercolor Days

The Rainbow's Edge

The Music

Primary Image

Tangible Dreams

Thumbprints in the Stream of Time

## Watercolor Days

It is a rain-soaked morning at seven a.m., when the clock on Julie's nightstand begins to sound. With her eyes still half-closed, she rolls over to cuddle with David, her husband of eight years. She feels the empty sheets beside her instead, and in a sleepy voice, utters his name.

"David?"

She sits up, and opens her eyes.

"David?"

Realizing that she is alone, a look of sadness falls over her face, and the emptiness swells within her. She falls back on the bed, hugs David's pillow, and begins to sob into it. After crying her heart out, Julie gets up to prepare for another day at Mercy Hospital.

Walking through the halls, Julie wrinkles her nose to the acrid smell, and quickens her pace to David's room. On the way, she passes people, some in wheelchairs, and some slowly walking with IV poles in tow. The noises all around become a deafening cacophony of buzzers, telephones, moaning, and orders.

With a backpack, two coffees, and a pastry bag in hand, she takes a deep breath, fights back the tears, and tries to composed herself, before entering Room 1204.

She finds David still sleeping, and walks to the table and chairs to set everything down. She looks over to see him lying almost motionless except for the painful flinching. Standing beside his bed, she brushes the hair from his face, revealing a pale hue with most of the color being in his beard.

It was only two years before, at the construction site David was in charge of, when the problem began. It was a hot summer day, and the popular tunes emanated from a nearby radio.

David looked up at the men on the beams, and shaded his eyes.

"Come on guys, let's hustle."

"Hey, we're going as fast as we can."

"What's the rush anyway?"

Rolling his eyes, David responds, "Well, in case you forgot, we do have a deadline to meet and you don't want to mess with the boss."

Shaking his head, he mumbles to himself in disbelief, "What's the rush?"

It was that night, the stress from the day got to him. David awakened from his dream with a painful cramp in his leg. He sits up in the dark, and grabs his leg while moaning, waking Julie. She rolls over, and turns on the light.

"David, what's wrong?"

"It's a cramp… in my leg again."

"It's been every night this week. Don't you think you should have it checked out?"

David rubbed his leg, and finally got some relief, although Julie could still see the pain on his face.

"No, it's just overworked muscles. We've been pushing to get this job finished in time."

He sat up, put his head back, closed his eyes, and sighed. Julie moved over, and put her head on his chest, closed her eyes, and kissed it. He looked down at her and put his hands through her hair.

"I'll bet your leg muscles aren't the only ones that are overworked," she said.

"You can say that again."

"Then turn over."

David looked at the alarm clock.

"Jules, it is three in the morning."

"And your point is? Come on, while I'm awake.

David reluctantly rolled over and closed his eyes, while Julie started to massage his shoulders.

"What did I ever do to deserve you, Jules?"

Julie leaned in and kissed his neck and back. He turned enough to put his arm around her and had her lay down next to him.

"I can't work on your shoulders from here, you know."

David enveloped her in his arms, they kissed, and he rolled over to shut the light.

Not wanting him to waste any more time, they set up an appointment with David's doctor. Julie sits impatiently in the waiting room. Just when she thinks that she can't stand it any longer, the nurse comes out.

"Mrs. Taylor?"

Julie gets up from her chair.

"Yes?"

"You can come in, and join your husband now."

They walk to Dr. Robard's office. The nurse opens the door to let Julie in, and then closes it on her way out. Dr. Robard gets up from leaning up against the desk, and shakes Julie's hand.

"Good to see you again Julie, although I wish it were under better circumstances. Please, have a seat."

Dr. Robard sits in his chair. Julie sits down, and looks at David, as he takes her hand in his.

David asks what they both are wondering.

"What is it Doc?"

Dr. Robard puts on his glasses, re-reads the MRI results, and then puts both down on the desk. Addressing them he says with a heavy heart, "David, Julie, I'm going to come right to the point. The pain and swelling in your leg is more than overworked muscles. From the MRI, it looks like a tumor. It is a small one, but it is a tumor."

David and Julie look from the doctor to each other, as their hands grip tighter.

"A small one, does that mean it isn't malignant, David questions.

"Not necessarily, but let's not make any conclusions until we've done some tests."

"What kind of tests," Julie asks.

"Well for starters, I'd like to do a biopsy."

"Biopsy, I don't like the sound of that."

"I'm not going to lie to you David. It isn't the most unpleasant test you could have, but it will be uncomfortable. Would you like me to explain the procedure?"

David looks to Julie to make sure that she is all right with hearing the details. She looks back and nods.

"Are you sure Jules?"

"Yes."

"We do what's called a core needle biopsy. You'll be awake but we'll freeze the area, and then use a thin needle to aspirate some fluid and small bone fragments."

"Why would there be bone fragments in the tumor?"

"That's a very legitimate question, David. The answer is because the tumor is in your bone.

Julie excitedly asks, "A tumor in the bone? But doesn't that mean it's ..."

Dr. Robard cuts her off mid-sentence.

"As I said, let's not make any definite conclusions right now until we see the results of the biopsy. I'd like to schedule you to go in on Friday afternoon. Will that be a problem?"

David answers half-dazed, "Friday? Sure. What time?"

"Two o'clock. Do either of you have any questions thus far?"

Both of them are still in shock and just look at one another.

"No, I guess not. This is going to take a while to sink in first," David says.

"Yes, I'm sure it will. If you do think of any questions, feel free to call."

David gets up first and shakes Dr. Robard's hand.

"Thank you, Dr. Robard."

David helps Julie out of her chair and steadies her.

"You can get all the necessary paperwork from the nurse on your way out."

They walk to the reception area, get the paperwork and their coats, then leave the office and go out into the street.

One week later David is back in Dr. Robard's office.

"So Doc. what are the results on the biopsy?"

"Well David, I wish I could give you better news."

David runs his hand across his face, and hangs his head. After a moment or two, he looks up at the doctor with anxiousness.

"Just give it to me straight Doc. You know I don't like beating around the bush. I need to know what I'm dealing with here."

"At this point, the tumor looks localized."

"So right now it doesn't seem to be anywhere else?"

"As far as we can tell, no it isn't. We'll set up the radiation sessions as soon as possible. This will help shrink it if not get rid of it altogether. We have a good chance of stopping it from spreading any further."

"Doc, I know we're not supposed to jump to any conclusions, but while Julie's not here I need to know something. Let's say hypothetically, that it has spread, what would be the next step?"

"Then we would have to operate. I'm sorry David. I do wish I had better news for you. Let's just pray that it hasn't spread and we can get it all with the radiation.

"Okay, whatever it takes. I just want to get rid of this and get on with my life."

After dinner, David is sitting at his desk in the den doing some research when Julie walks in. He minimizes what he is looking at on the computer screen and pulls up the bank's website instead. Julie walks behind him and starts massaging his shoulders.

"What are you doing, honey?"

"Nothing much, just getting some bills out of the way."

"Oh. I have to run over to my parents' to drop off some clothes for Nicky, so he'll be all set for tomorrow. It will only be a half-hour or so. Did you want to come with me?"

"No, it's ok, you go, and I'll finish up some things here."

"Are you sure?"

"Yes, I'll be fine. No worries."

Julie kisses him and says, "Okay, I'll be back."

David gets up and walks to the window when he hears the car engine. He watches Julie drive away, and then turns around to pour himself a drink. Putting the stereo on a normal volume, he takes a sip, and turns back to the window to stare out into the darkness. His facial expression slowly changes to anger. After another sip, he cranks up the volume on the stereo, and his body begins to stiffen. Taking the third sip, he starts to shake as he tries to fight the anxiety and tears that are welling up within him.

The glass drops from his hand, and shatters on the floor. Crouching down to clean it up, one of the shards cuts his hand. He holds it out, and watches the blood pool in his palm.

Closing his hand to make a fist, he falls back and finally breaks down, the sound of which goes unheard, drowned out by the music. The song ends and he screams.

When Julie comes home she sees the small light on in the den, and goes in to find David asleep on the couch. The glass and blood are gone, so she doesn't have any idea of what took place in the short time she was gone. She begins to cover him and he opens his eyes. Julie can see David has been crying.

He moves over so that she can sit with him and he places his head in her lap. Without words, she strokes his head, gliding her fingers through his hair. Emotionally drained, the tears run silently down his face until he falls asleep. Julie's tears fall simultaneously.

The ride to the hospital is a quiet one, as David keeps his eyes and thoughts fixed on the early morning traffic. Julie stares out the window, only occasionally turning to look at David.

They arrive and drive around the dizzying turns in the underground parking garage. The elevator emits some unnerving sounds as it climbs to the oncology department on the ninth floor.

The older nurse at the admitting desk greets them with a half-smile.

"Good morning. Could I have your name please?"

"David Taylor.

"What is your date of birth, Mr. Taylor?"

"February 8, 1972."

"Could I have your insurance card please?"

David takes out his wallet, searches for the card, and then hands it to her. She makes a copy of it, hands it back to him, finishes writing on the form, and looks up.

"If you'll just have a seat, Mr. and Mrs. Taylor, someone will be here momentarily to draw some blood."

An intern walks over to them right after they sit down.

"Mr. Taylor if you would follow me please."

David has his blood drawn, then he goes back to sit with Julie. Feeling his anxiety, Julie puts her hand in his and squeezes it.

"We're going to get through this together honey."

David just nods his head in agreement. As he sits there waiting, he can hear the nurses making appointments and other patients conversing with family members. He begins to zone out so that all the sounds become mixed, becoming something in the distance. He hears Julie calling his name but it sounds like it is coming from far away.

"David?"

All at once, he becomes alert to her voice.

"What?"

"It's your turn, Mr. Taylor if you could follow me please."

David follows her into the treatment room as if he were walking in a dream. The room has a very aesthetic atmosphere. Every one of his senses heightened as his surroundings start to make everything surreal.

He undresses, and covered only by a paper gown, he sits on the cold metal table; feeling exposed mentally as well as physically. The light, sterile equipment, stark white walls, and the medicinal smell make him sick even before the treatment begins. He looks around, only to see more cold metal objects, gloves, and the faulty light on the X-ray wall-unit flickering. The whirring sound of the machine seems to get louder and louder until it makes him want to jump out of his skin. Just as he can't stand it any longer, the technician comes into the room, startling him.

"Good morning, Mr. Taylor. My name is Derek."

In a quiet, almost inaudible voice, David responds.

"Hey."

"Any questions before we begin?"

"Um, no, I guess not."

"Okay, then let's get you started with the procedure."

A week later, Dr. Robard gives David the results that the radiation dissolved the tumor.

However, after only a year of being pain-free, David finds himself back in the doctor's office facing the news of a possible reoccurrence.

"I think the best course of action now is to do what's called a radionuclide bone scan."

"A radio what?"

"Radionuclide bone scan, it's a procedure where we inject a radioactive substance into the veins. The tumor absorbs the material and shows up as a dark spot. From this, we can see if it has spread beyond the bone itself."

"You're going to put radioactive material in me?"

"Yes, it's a procedure that has proven to be very useful."

"I guess I don't have any other choice then, do I?"

"Unfortunately not, we'll know right away, so I'll come and give you the results."

Two hours later David and Dr. Robard are sitting back in the office. Dr. Robard takes off his glasses and places them on the desk. He rubs his eyes, then clasps his hands together and places them on the desk.

"David, I don't know what to say. I don't understand but it's returned."

"Oh God not again, how bad is it this time?"

"It's what we call osteosarcoma. It spread into the nearby tissue and muscle. We're looking at surgery, and chemotherapy."

"Both? Can't we just do the surgery?"

"I'm afraid not. We have to treat it aggressively because that's how it's fighting against you."

In the hospital room, David is nervously waiting for the injection of sodium pentothal to put him to sleep for the operation. The nurse finally comes in, gives him the shot, and then leaves. As much as he tries to fight the feeling of the anesthesia overtaking his body, dragging him down into the darkness, and leaving him with the fear of not emerging from its effects, it is useless.

When he begins to regain consciousness an hour later, the blackness swirls around in his head. He hears voices calling his name, telling him to wake up. He has to force himself to climb out of the abyss and into the light appearing above him.

"Dr. Robard?"

"It looks like we got all of it, David. The treatments will take care of anything small we might have missed. That way we're ahead of it, just in case there's any hiding on us."

David closes his eyes and breathes a sigh of relief.


David and Julie walk across the hospital lobby to the elevators. They make their way up to the ninth floor, the oncology department, and its admission desk. The nurse greets them.

"Good morning Mr. and Mrs. Taylor."

"Good morning Anna," they both reply.

David well knows the procedure and walks to the station where his blood will be drawn. As the intern Chris finishes, and is about to walk with David to the treatment area, he asks,

"Where would you like to sit today, Mr. Taylor?"

Unenthused, David answers, "Over by the window I guess."

"An excellent choice, will Mrs. Taylor be joining you?"

David, becoming agitated, responds, "You're making it sound like I have a dinner engagement at a restaurant."

"I'm sorry Mr. Taylor. I…"

"It's just that this is sapping all my energy and patience. I realize that you're trying to make this lousy situation easier to deal with, but I'm sorry, it's not working."

"I've been doing this for a while, so I understand the roller-coaster ride of emotions. It starts with shock and denial before the anger and depression set in, and then for some, acceptance."

"Have you ever experienced it?"

"No… I."

"Then how can you tell me about acceptance? It's not acceptable. How can anyone just sit back and accept it? I refuse to accept that this miserable force will take over my life."

"That positive attitude will work as a plus in your favor. Your family's support will help strengthen you too. So let's get this over with."

Chris gets the I.V. set up, and then moves to another patient who needs attending to.

David watches some of the other patients, and catches the eye of a young woman who smiles at him. He returns the smile with a half-hearted one.

"Hi, I'm Susan Parker."

"Hi. David Taylor."

"I don't think I've seen you here before. Is this your first time?"

"No, actually it's my second round of treatments."

"Same here, hopefully, it will be the last."

"That's what I'm hoping for too."

"You seem to have an optimistic outlook on things though. You do need that to survive."

"You think I have an optimistic outlook? Not exactly, I just don't want someone who's never been through this to tell me what my emotions are going to be, or should be, that's all. How can you have an optimistic outlook when you know what it's doing to you?"

"It hasn't won yet and I'm not going to let it either. You're fighting it if you're here. If you don't fight it here (points to her head) and here, (points to her heart) then you might as well not take any treatment because it's already beat you. You've made it easier for it to overtake you. Look at all that you have to be grateful for, do you have a wife?"

"Yes."

"Do you have any children?"

"One, a little boy named Nicholas.

"Then take advantage of every waking moment, so that if it does win in the end, and there's no guarantee that it will, you can honestly say that you gave everything to them and fought against it as long and as hard as you could. Don't let it take your dignity from you too. It's bad enough that it robs us of most of our time, energy, sleep, and, she pauses, our hair."

Both release a semi-laugh at the last item mentioned.

"Have you always felt this strongly about fighting it," David asks.

"No. I went through all the other emotions too. I was very angry at first. I would sit and look at pictures of when I was healthy until I cried. Then I went through I went what I call the "what I had" syndrome. I had long hair down to my waist at one time. I loved brushing it at night before I went to bed. I had a promising career as a model. I had a fiancé too. After my diagnoses, and he couldn't handle it. He left and eventually called off the wedding. I guess he thought I would be less of a woman after a double mastectomy."

"I'm sorry, I didn't realize it."

"Don't be sorry, I'm not. It changed my thinking and helped me set priorities for the more important things."

"What made you change all that?"

"When I was going for the first treatment after the operation there was this little girl, Anna. She was about seven. She had already been through so much between operations and chemo. What amazed me is how she was more worried about how her mom was going to be after she died. She was so brave and positive when her mother was there, but at night, she would break down and cry until she fell asleep. I went in some nights and stayed with her until she fell asleep."

"Did she...?"

"Yes, it was after I had left the hospital. I went to visit her several times. One day about two months later, I went to see her and the nurses told me that she had died only a few hours before. Her mother had left a card thanking me for being there for her daughter."

"I guess this filthy disease has no boundaries. Seven years old. She never even got a chance to see what a normal child's life was, never mind what it could have offered her when she was older. It sucks and I hate it with every part of me, for her, you, me, and everyone else it affects, including our families."

"I hate it just as much as you do, but we can't let that hate eat away at what we have left to give until there's nothing to us but empty shells."

Susan reaches for her tote bag. She takes out a bookmarker and hands it to David. He takes it from her, and looks at it.

"What's this?"

"It's just one of the philosophies I try to live by. I make these bookmarkers and cards with different positive quotes on them. I give them out to other patients and their family members. Sometimes it helps to build us up when we need it the most."

"'Every second we live is a new and unique moment of the universe, a moment that never was before and never will be again.' Pablo Casals. Well, that's certainly a positive thought. Thanks."

"You're welcome."

Julie walks into the room and over to David.

"Hey."

"Hey. Jules, this is Susan Parker."

"It's nice to meet you, Susan. I'm Julie Taylor.

Julie looks at the bookmarker still in David's hand.

"What's that?"

"Oh, Susan makes bookmarkers and cards with quotes that can help us keep a positive attitude, or in my case, *get* a positive attitude."

"Well it doesn't happen overnight, but I think you're headed in the right direction."

"Thanks."

Both David and Susan shake hands as if they were signing a pact.

At home, Julie is in the hallway outside the bathroom door and can hear David vomiting from the chemotherapy. After several times, he stops. Julie walks in and sees him slumped against the wall, sweating profusely, his hair soaked.

Julie wets a facecloth in cold water, and wipes his face and neck. He puts his head into her as she holds him. Without any words spoken, Julie helps him get up, and lean on her as they walk into the bedroom. She helps him into the bed. He falls back on the pillows, all his strength drained from his limp body.

With labored breathing, David whispers, "Julie, I can't do this anymore. I'm tired of being sick. I have no strength. I just want it to end."

Julie's eyes start to fill up and she turns away from him.

"I'm sorry Julie but it hurts so much. Almost as much as it hurts to know that, I'm never going to be with you and Nicholas anymore. I hate being this way and you having to see it and take care of me. What good am I? I'm useless, nothing but a burden!"

David leans back and bangs his head against the headboard. Julie turns and faces him.

"What good are you? Whether you realize or not, you *are* the same loving husband that you've always been. You still have a warm personality. Even the way your whole face lights up when you get excited about something that has meaning to you."

Her voice starts to crack. "I love to hear your voice first thing in the morning and the last thing at night. I feel safe with you here."

"How can I make you feel safe? I lay here helpless! You do everything for me! I consider that a burden. It's not right!" He slams his fist into the bed and starts coughing.

"A burden, I hate what this disease is doing to you, but I am your wife and I want to do what I can for you because I love you!"

The tears flow freely as Julie is still facing him. David takes her face in his hand, and he is crying too. He pulls her to him.

"I know, and I love you too Jules."


As Susan reads the letter, which has just arrived, she can hear David's voice and see the images outlined in the letter.

Susan,

How are you feeling? I hope that you are better than the last time we spoke. Have you finished reading the rest of your novel? What was the name of it again? Did you get Julie's care package? She's something else, isn't she? I love her so much it hurts. How's your mom doing? Did she win at BINGO again this week?

I've started keeping a journal, for mental clarity I guess, instead of the mental turmoil that exists in me. The emotional baggage and intense anxiety attacks are physically draining. The darkness in my soul seems to appear more frequently these days. It's like being at the bottom of a pit - I can see the light above, but the more I try to climb up towards it, the more the sides collapse in and push me further down.

I do try to look for the brighter moments to cherish though, as you suggested. My desk is by the window facing the front yard. A squirrel is trying to take the food away from the birds at the feeder in the yard. They're making quite a fuss over it too. Can't say I blame them any. So many things we take for granted until we have time to sit down and enjoy them.

We bought Nicky a puppy yesterday. You should see him playing with it. He giggles like crazy when it licks his face. When we get the pictures developed, I'll send them to you. He's growing up so fast Susan. I can't believe I'm not going to be around to see it.

Listening to music helps to block out some of the pain. Some days it's classical, other days it's country or the oldies. It seems to go with whatever mood I happen to be in at the time.

I look in the mirror and don't even recognize myself anymore. The loss of appetite doesn't do too much for weight gain. I better get back to weight lifting huh," he laughs.

Even though I haven't eaten much for weeks, today I had a craving for a hamburger, fries, and a milkshake. Susan, you should have seen the look on Julie's face when I told her that! She ran right out and got it before I had a chance to change my mind. I didn't finish it all, but what I did have of it was great. I'd forgotten what those things tasted like.

Well, I guess I'll leave it here for now. Looking forward to hearing from you. Take care. Julie says hi. Say hello to your mom for us.

David

Susan writes her return letter.

David,

I sit alone in the darkness tonight, with only the dim light from the lamp on my nightstand. Anything stronger seems to bother my eyes now.

The rain is pouring down and tapping against my window. It starts as a gentle mist. Steadily it intensifies, and then just as quickly diminishes, until it is soft again. Within a moment it has heightened again, this time bring the light with it. It fills the room for just a split second, and then it is gone, leaving the sky pitch black once more. I only get to count to three before the deafening roar of thunder crashes overhead.

The sound of the wind makes me shiver. This battle, taking place within me, is like the wind-swept rain. I have as much control over it, as the rain has over the wind. Again, I shiver as I see what I have just written. A cold settles deep in my soul.

There are days when I can be happy and positive, others the pain is too great, and the depression sets in. I hate those days. Unfortunately, they are the ones that seem to appear more often now. I think of Anna and how she is resting, free of pain. These days, I wonder why it couldn't be me instead.

I apologize for not writing an encouraging letter. It's just not in me today. I know you'll understand.

I hope that this letter will find you in better spirits, and that it doesn't diminish them.

Your friend always, Susan

Three months later, David is sitting in Nicholas' bedroom, reading him 'Goodnight, Moon'. At the end of the story, Nicholas is almost asleep, so David sings one of the songs he wrote for him, and has sung to him since he was born. Nicholas falls asleep. David tucks him in and walks out of the room, leaving the door slightly ajar.

He limps downstairs to the kitchen where Julie is doing the dishes. David comes up behind her, puts his arms around her waist, and kisses her on the head.

"Is Nicky asleep?"

"Yes, but only after a story and his song."

"Let me guess, 'Goodnight Moon'?"

"It was, as usual."

"Do you think he'll ever get sick of that story?"

"Hopefully, before we get tired of reading it."

"Maybe we should get him some Dr. Seuss books."

"Sounds like a plan, maybe 'Green Eggs and Ham'."

"You're a poet and you don't know it."

"Actually, I do, but thanks for noticing my almost hidden talent."

He squeezes her and kisses her again.

"Do you know you're as beautiful now as the day I met you?"

"Well I don't know about that, but I do know you're just as handsome."

They reminisce about that day, ten years earlier.

They were at a bonfire at the end of August. Everyone was sitting around making s'mores, playing word games, and laughing. David was sitting on a large rock with his guitar leaning against it. Julie was sitting diagonally from him, roasting marshmallows, and laughing with the girl sitting next to her. The boy sitting next to David slapped him on the back.

"Hey David, play something for us will you?"

Everyone was still talking and laughing, until David started to play. He joked around at first with several tunes just to warm everyone up. They all joined in singing while he played. While everyone was in a good mood, David took a chance and played the new song he wrote.

Shyly, he said, "Well I haven't quit my day job yet, but tell me what you think of this."

He self-consciously started to sing a love song, without really looking at anyone. After the first verse, he began to calm down. By the last verse, he stole a glance at Julie, long enough to catch her eye and nail the song. It blew everyone away. They all began clapping and talking all at once.

"Wow! That was awesome! Did you write that?"

"Yeah, but like I said I haven't quit my day job", he laughed.

He stole another look at Julie, this time longer, and looked for her reaction to the song. She smiled and nodded to show her approval. He returned her smile in gratitude.

One of the other girls asked, "Is that the only one you've written? Can you sing us another one?"

"Maybe in a few minutes, right now I need a drink of water."

David got up and went to the cooler for a bottle of water. Julie made her way to him. She loved his attire; he had on a black t-shirt with a denim shirt over it, black jeans, and cowboy boots.

"You were wonderful just now."

David turned to her and was equally fond of her attire, as it was almost a carbon copy of his, only feminine. She was wearing a bandana, placed over her long blond hair, a denim half-shirt tied in the front over a black t-shirt, black jeans, and cowboy boots.

"You think so?"

"I wouldn't say if I didn't. By the way, I'm Julie Smith."

"Well thank you, Julie Smith. It is a pleasure to meet you. I'm David Taylor."

"Hey Dave, come on we're all waiting to hear another song."

"Yeah, come on."

David turned to the crowd.

"Okay, Okay. I'm coming."

He turned back to Julie.

"Care to join me?"

Ten months after the surgery, Julie finds herself right back to where she was at the beginning of this devastating ordeal, walking through Mercy hospital.

Reaching the end of the hall, Julie wrinkles her nose to the acrid smell and quickens her pace to David's room. On the way, she passes people, some in wheelchairs, and some walking slowly, with IV poles in tow. The noises all around become a deafening cacophony of buzzers, telephones, and moaning.

With a backpack, two coffees, and a pastry bag in hand, she takes a deep breath, fights back the tears, and tries to compose herself before entering Room 1204. She finds David still sleeping, and walks to the table and chairs to set everything down. She looks over to see him lying almost motionless except for the painful flinching. Standing beside his bed, she brushes the hair from his face, revealing a pale hue with most of the color being in his beard. She watches him sleep as the tears run down her face.

David softly moans, and Julie's concentration is broken. She reaches over to feel his fevered brow. David slowly opens his eyes to look at her.

"I'm right here."

She caresses his hands. He gives her a faint smile, assuring her that he knows, but the pain in his eyes stabs her heart.

"Are you feeling any better today?"

"A little, how about you, did you get any sleep last night?"

"Some. Teasingly, she says, "I did have a good dream about you though."

"Really, you'll have to fill me I, was I good?"

"You were great, as always."

She leans over him and they kiss.

"My dad wants to bring Nicholas in around one. Is that all right?"

"Do you think it's a good idea for him to see me like this?"

"He misses you terribly, David."

"I miss him too, but…"

The orderly comes in with the lunch tray.

"Here you are, Mr. Taylor."

After the orderly leaves, David tries to sit up to eat, but has trouble, and becomes frustrated. Julie tries to help.

"It's okay, I can do it. It just takes me a while.

He continues to pull himself up.

"I can help you."

She starts to help him.

David reacts and says rather roughly, "I said I can do it myself."

Julie lets go of his arm and backs up while trying not to look hurt.

"I'm sorry. I didn't mean to yell at you. I just won't accept being an invalid. I want to do as much as I can for as long as I can Julie."

"It's all right. I'm sorry."

David's hand starts to shake as he picks up the fork. He steadies it and manages one bite. The second portion falls off onto the front of his shirt. He slams the fork down and pushes the tray away.

"You know what? I'm not hungry anyway. Besides, have you tasted this? Hospital food isn't the greatest you know."

"I can go and get you something from the restaurant next door."

"No, but maybe later; thanks."

David looks over at the pastry bag and coffee cups on the table.

"That bag wouldn't have anything good in it by any chance, would it?"

"As a matter of fact, it does, since it is from our favorite bakery."

Julie gets the bag and gives it to him. David takes out a cinnamon doughnut and savors the first bite.

"Do you remember when that shop first opened, Jules?"

"It wasn't there when we went on our honeymoon, and when we got back, there it was on the corner. The first Sunday we were home you went there and we were hooked from then on."

They reminisce how David came in with lattes, raspberry pastries, and the newspaper, and brought them to Jules to have breakfast in bed. Julie put them aside while David climbed into bed. He tickled her, which turned into a pillow fight.

"We had some fun times together, Jules."

Both of them get a far-away look in their eyes, remembering the days at the zoo, and then the park when it started to rain and they ran for the gazebo. David picked her up, swung her around, and kissed her.

David speaks first and says, "And then came that day in my life, the one I never thought possible."

Julie was single and living in her parents' house, when on one particularly stormy afternoon she looked out the upstairs window and saw David running up the street. She grabbed a towel from the linen closet and ran downstairs to meet him at the door, just as he rang the bell.

Soaking wet and shivering, he came into the entryway, and Julie helped him take off his coat.

"Come in before you catch pneumonia. Where is your car?"

Trying to catch his breath, he managed to say, "It gave out about sixteen blocks back."

David took off his boots.

"And you ran all that way in the pouring rain, are you crazy?"

"I'm crazy in love with you."

They kissed. As he was still shivering, the water dripped from his hair onto Julie. As she hung his coat on the rack, David quickly reached into one of the pockets, pulled out a ring box, and opened it.

"This is how crazy I am for you. Will you marry me?"

"Yes!"

She jumped up and hugged him.

Their wedding was on a beautiful Saturday morning in February. The minister stood before them, instructing them about their new roles as husband and wife.

"Proverbs chapter 31 asks, 'Who can find a capable wife? Her value is far more than that of corals. Her husband trusts her from his heart. She should be industrious and hardworking. Kindness is found in her. Her husband and children will praise her. She remembers that charm and beauty are fleeting but the secret person of the heart remains and is an important quality.'

"This is part of your role Julie. Ephesians chapter 5 tells us, 'Let wives be in subjection to their husbands as to the Lord, because a husband is head of his wife just as the Christ is head of the congregation. In fact, as the congregation is in subjection to the Christ, wives should also be to their husbands in everything. The wife should have deep respect for her husband.'

In addition, David, the same chapter tells husbands to 'continue loving your wife, just as the Christ also loved the congregation and gave himself up for it. In the same way, husbands should love their wives as their own bodies. A man who loves his wife loves himself, for no man ever hated his own body, but he feeds and cherishes it. For this reason, a man will leave his father and his mother and he will stick to his wife, and the two will be one flesh.' In other words, a husband seeks his wife's welfare ahead of his own. When making decisions, take her views and thoughts into consideration *beforehand,* and value her input. Never ignore or neglect her.

"Keeping in mind the seriousness of marriage, remember, when you both vow to take each other as married partners, you are promising to accept each other with not only their virtues but also with their faults. You will discover new aspects of each other's personalities, and there will at times be disappointments. Don't let the sun set without resolving any differences between you. Moreover, in love, make allowances for one another, especially as you spoke these solemn vows or promises in God's sight. Do not take these vows lightly, but rather, very seriously.

"Ecclesiastes chapter four gives us a beautiful word picture of how marriage should be. It says, 'Two are better than one because they have a good reward for their hard work. For if one of them falls, the other can help his partner up. But what will happen to the one who falls with no one to help him up? Moreover, if two lie down together, they will stay warm, but how can just one keep warm? And someone may overpower one alone, but two together can take a stand against him. And a threefold cord cannot quickly be torn apart.' God is the third cord in your marriage. If you both wrap yourselves around him, so to speak, he will strengthen your marriage and make it so strong that no one or nothing can destroy it.

"We also mentioned that love is the driving force in the marriage and can help us to make allowances for each other when appropriate. Another familiar scripture, which outlines the quality of love, and how it molds us to action, is 1 Corinthians chapter 13. Please take note of the perfect description of love.

'Love is patient and kind. Love is not jealous. It does not brag, does not get puffed up, does not behave indecently, does not look for its own interests, and does not become provoked. It does not keep account of the injury. It does not rejoice over unrighteousness, but rejoices with the truth. It bears all things, believes all things, hopes all things, endures all things. Love never fails.'

Marriage is a gift; cherish it. If you read the scriptures together every day and allow them to guide you in life, you will be able to live up to your vows. Set aside time each day to talk to each other. Serve God *together*, study his word *together*. Take time to walk *together*, sit *together*, and eat *together*. Enjoy life *together*! Be kind to one another, love and cherish one another, be tenderly compassionate. Remember, respect in a marriage is mutual; it is earned, we do not demand it.

"And now, if you will both stand, and hold hands, we will have you say your vows. Julie, you go first, so if you will please repeat after me.

"I, Julie Nadine Smith take you, David James Taylor, to be my wedded husband."

"I, Julie Nadine Smith take you, David James Taylor, to be my wedded husband."

"To love, cherish, and deeply respect in accordance with the divine law, as set forth in the Holy Scriptures for Christian wives."

"To love, cherish, and deeply respect in accordance with the divine law…"

Julie nervously laughed, as she forgot the rest. David smiled and squeezed her hands.

The minister jumped in to help her, "As set forth in the Holy Scriptures for Christian wives."

"As set forth in the Holy Scriptures for Christian wives."

"For as long as we both shall live together on earth,"

"For as long as we both shall live together on earth,"

"According to God's marital arrangement."

"According to God's marital arrangement."

"Very good, and now, it's your turn, David."

"I, David James Taylor take you, Julie Nadine Smith, to be my wedded wife."

"I, David James Taylor take you, Julie Nadine Smith, to be my wedded wife."

"To love and cherish in accordance with the divine law,"

"To love and cherish in accordance with the divine law,"

"As set forth in the Holy Scriptures for Christian husbands."

"As set forth in the Holy Scriptures for Christian husbands."

"For as long as we both shall live together on earth,"

"For as long as we both shall live together on earth,"

"According to God's marital arrangement."

"According to God's marital arrangement."

"Wonderfully done, David; you can thank your wife for already making life easier for you."

They laughed along with the minister and the congregation.

David mouthed the words 'thank you' to Julie.

The minister continued, "You may exchange rings at this time. Before God and those present, who have been witnesses to your solemn promises, I now pronounce you husband and wife. You may kiss the bride."

At the reception, everyone stood up and applauded, as the master of ceremonies announced their arrival.

"Ladies and gentlemen, it is my pleasure to announce the new couple, Mr. and Mrs. David Taylor."

David and Julie entered the room waving, and walked to the table set for the bridal party.

Once everyone had finished eating, the M.C. approached the microphone to make a request.

"Could we please have the bride and groom come up for the first dance please?"

'Endless Love' was their special song, and the newly married couple danced across the floor like silk gliding across glass. Lost in each other eyes, they were oblivious to anything going on around them.

As the song came to the end, David took Julie in his arms, kissed her, and whispered, "Now, you're not only my dance partner Mrs. Taylor, but my life partner as well."

"Forever."

"Forever."

Everyone clapped, and before David and Julie could walk away, the M.C. made a second request.

"Can Mr. and Mrs. Kenneth Smith come to the dance floor, please?"

The band played 'Look at Us' for them.

After a night of dancing and spending time with their friends, they made their way to the table, in the center of the dance floor. They cut and fed each other a piece of wedding cake, and the band began to play the final song of the night. As they danced, the guests formed a circle around them, so that when they finished, they could go to each one and say their goodbyes.

They drove to their mountain cabin for the week honeymoon. The snow began to fall as they arrived. David took the first of the suitcases out of the trunk, and handed it to Julie. When she didn't take it from him, he looked behind, only to see her spinning around as the tiny, white flakes fell over her. He stood there laughing, and then he put the suitcase back on the seat, and joined her, by picking her up and spinning her around.

Once settled in the cabin, they sat on the floor in front of the fireplace with a bottle of champagne. Gazing into David's eyes, Julie asked, "Do you remember the song you sang to me the night we got engaged?"

"Absolutely, it was and is the song that said everything I wanted to say to you."

"Can you sing it for me now?"

David held her close and sang 'Lady' to her. When he finished, Julie's eyes were sparkling. The passion rose, and they made love, as the flames danced in the fireplace.

After reliving those beautiful memories, David looks longing at Julie.

"God, how I wish we could repeat that night, right now. I miss you, Jules. You don't know *how badly* I miss you."

Julie runs her slender fingers across his chest and bites her lip so as not to cry.

"Yes, I do, because I miss you just as much."

There is silence for a few seconds before David breaks it.

"I see you're wearing the pearls I bought you for our first anniversary."

"That night was special too, wasn't it?"

"It certainly was; I especially remember that little black dress that you were wearing. I wanted to forget all about the dinner reservations and stay home and celebrate with you right then and there."

"Is that so? Well, I might add that you looked so strikingly handsome in that suit, that I was thinking the same thing."

"Were you really, Mrs. Taylor?"

"I was, but then we got caught up in giving each other our gifts that it was time to leave."

"Yes, I remember you were sitting at your vanity table when I came in the room. You didn't even see me come up behind you. I think you might have jumped when I asked what you were doing."

"I was focused on finding the right jewelry to wear, when you took a box from behind your back and said, "Well, you could try these.""

"And your eyes lit up as if I had just given you the moon, and you hadn't even opened the box yet to see what was in it. I should have put a ring from the gumball machine in there to trick you," David laughs.

"David!"

"You are beautiful Jules. You still outshine those pearls like you did that night."

Julie blushes.

"Wow, I can still make you blush. Am I good or am I good?"

"You're great."

"You're pretty great yourself. Those tickets to the basketball game for me and Jason to have a guy's night out were very cool."

"And don't forget how we both picked out the same card for each other?"

"Now that was awesome."

"I remember you said it just shows you how in sync we were with one another besides when we're dancing."

"We still are too."

"We sure are."

"Do you remember the song that I dedicated to you that night?"

"How could I forget? It was 'Something That We Do'. We sang the last lines to one another."

"Remember how they go?"

"I do."

They sing them to each other.

"There is no request too big or small. We give ourselves; we give our all. Love isn't some place that we fall. It's something that we do."

"That was such a wonderful evening."

"Yes, especially dancing with you. We were lost in time. Everything else around us just disappeared. It was just you and me that night."

"Not counting everyone who saw me crying."

"But they were tears of joy weren't they?"

"Of course they were."

"Well then, those are the best kind of tears."

David pauses.

"I'm glad we've always been there for one another."

"Yes, especially when things got rough."

"And we did have some tough times."

"That's when the other kind of tears appeared."

David's drive home on that winter night was brutal, and when he came in the house, he found Julie curled up in a comforter on the couch, crying. David quickly took off his boots and coat and rushed over to her.

"Baby, what's wrong?"

Julie cried even more.

"Did you have to say that?"

"What? What did I say? I only asked you what was wrong."

"You said baby," she sobbed.

"I thought you liked it when I called you that?"

"Not anymore."

"Jules will you please tell me what's wrong?"

"The doctor said I couldn't have any babies."

David took her in his arms and held her tightly.

"Oh honey, I'm so sorry. I didn't mean to make it worse. Its okay, we'll work through this. I love you and nothing is going to change that."

"We proved him wrong though didn't we?"

"We certainly did. One year later we were in the maternity ward holding our newborn son."

"What do you want to name him?"

"What do you think about the name Nicholas?"

"Nicholas always was my favorite name."

"We did it. We sure surprised everyone."

"Yes, we did. What do doctors know anyway?"
Julie puts her head on David's chest and he kisses her head.

"And now we're waiting for another little one."

Doctor Hanson walks in with the equipment to do a sonogram.

"Speaking of which…," Julie says.

"What's all this?"

"Dr. Hanson agreed to do the sonogram here, so you can be with me."

"What, really?"

He kisses Julie again.

"I love you, Jules. You don't know how much this means to me. Dr. Hanson, thank you for doing this."

"You're certainly welcome. Now let's get you ready Julie."

Julie gets on the gurney next to David's bed and they do the sonogram while holding hands. It reveals that they are going to have a girl.

"So what do you think Mr. Taylor? You're going to be the proud father of a baby girl. Have you two picked out any names yet?"

Julie looks over to David to see his eyes fill up with tears, which makes her cry too.

"We had talked about the name Jocelyn," David says.

"I was thinking of giving her your mother's first name for her middle name."

"Jocelyn Elyse Taylor. That has a nice ring to it."

"I would have to agree."

David continues to stare at his daughter. Julie squeezes his hand, and he responds by squeezing it in return but continues looking at the monitor. Dr. Hanson looks at the two of them with sad tears in their eyes and turns away to capture the baby's image for the photograph.

As soon as Doctor Hanson leaves, Julie's father comes in holding Nicholas' hand. When Nicholas catches sight of his father, he breaks free, runs to his side, and tries to climb up on the bed.

"Daddy!"

"Hey, buddy. Come here."

Kenneth picks him up, and Julie cautions him as he sits next to David.

"Go slow, Nicky. Remember what we talked about this morning?"

"Yep, I member."

Julie's dad leans over and kisses her on the head.

"My girl."

"Daddy I made a picture for you. Want to see?"

"I sure do. Where is it?"

"Grandpa has it. Don't you, Grandpa?"

"Yes, I do. Here it is."

He hands the picture to Nicholas, and rests his hand on David's leg.

"You're looking better today son."

"Thanks, dad, how are you holding up?"

"Still well enough to bother your mother-in-law while she's trying to get things done around the house," he laughs.

David shakes his head and rolls his eyes.

"It's a good thing she loves you dad, or else you'd never get away with half of the things you do to her."

They all laugh.

David picks up the picture and starts to examine it while it is upside down.

"All right, let's see this picture of yours. Hmm, what is this?"

"Daddy you're silly. It goes this way."

They turn the picture right side up.

"Oh yes, of course, it does."

Nicholas sees the green Jello on David's tray.

"Daddy, can I have your Jello?"

"How about telling me what you've made here first, okay?"

"Okay. This is you and me fishing."

"I'm in the boat but where are you?"

"This is me in the water."

"What are you doing in the water? Aren't you supposed to be in the boat with me?"

"I was but I fell out of the boat. See, you're trying to get me with the fishing pole."

"Well, that's a great picture and story buddy, thank you. I think next time we'll make sure you don't fall out of the boat though. I don't want to lose you, you know."

"I don't want to lose you either Daddy. We'll be buddies forever right?"

Everyone's eyes start to fill up as they realize the import of Nicholas' question.

"Yep, buddies forever Nicky."

Nicholas starts to eat the Jello as if the mood hasn't changed.

"This is good Jello Dad. Want some?"

"No thanks, buddy, I saved it for you. I know how much you like it."

"Specially green right, cuz that's our favorite color."

"That's right. Dad, would you hang Nicky's picture up on the corkboard please?"

"Sure, we don't want any of that Jello to spill on it now, do we?"

"Speaking of pictures, look at the one I have."

Julie shows the sonogram picture to her father.

"It's official. It's a girl," David proudly proclaims.

"Who's a girl? Can I see it?"

"It's a picture of your baby sister."

"That's what my sister looks like? She doesn't look much like a baby."

"Well, she will. She's not done growing yet."

The orderly comes in to collect the lunch tray.

"Well, I see someone is eating the best part of this lunch."

He pats Nicholas on the head and messes up his hair.

"Yep, my dad saved it all for me, right dad?"

"That's right son, I did."

"Your dad must really love you if he gave up his Jello."

"He does. You can take this now. I'm all done."

"Already, wow that was fast. I don't think I know anyone who can eat Jello that fast."

"That's cuz I'm the fastest Jello eater in the world. It gives me muscles. See?"

"Wow! You must eat a lot of it to get those muscles."

"Every day, right Mom?

"Almost every day honey."

"Mom, can we go to the store and get Daddy the surprise now?"

Julie whispers audibly, "If it's going to be a surprise, we can't let him know about it, remember?"

Nicholas whispers loudly in Julie's direction,

"Oh yeah, I forgot."

He turns back to David.

"You didn't hear me, dad, did you?"

"We're you talking to me? I thought you were whispering to your mom. Is it a secret?"

"Yep, but I can't tell you because it's a surprise. Can we go now, Mom?"

"I'm ready."

"I'll be right back, okay dad?"

"Okay. I'll be right here waiting for you."

"Grandpa, are you coming too?"

"No, I think I'll stay here and talk to your dad so he won't be lonely."

"Okay. We'll be right back."

After they leave, Kenneth brings a chair to David's bedside.

"Dad, I want to tell you something before they come back. I just want to tell you how much I appreciate all that you've done for me over the years. You and Elyse took me in as your own. I'm glad that I could always come to you whenever I had a problem or just needed to talk. It's meant a great deal to me."

"Elyse and I are very proud of you, son. We couldn't have asked for anyone better for Julie."

Elyse walks into the room.

"I hope I'm not interrupting anything."

"Dad was just telling me how's he's been giving you a hard time. I told him to be careful or there'd be heck to pay."

Elyse walks over and kisses David on the head.

"You've got that right."

She hands him a box of dark chocolate covered cherries.

"Thanks, Mom."

"You're welcome. I figured you might want something sweet since you didn't get to eat your Jello."

"Boy, news travels quickly around this place."

Kenneth gets up and offers the chair to Elyse. She takes it with some apprehension, as she keeps her eye on him while she sits down.

"What are you looking at me like that for? I didn't do anything."

"Maybe not but I need to have eyes behind my head with you around. I never know what you're up to."

Kenneth whispers audibly to David, "You see, even when I'm being nice I get in trouble."

"You never mind that. Just because I'm old doesn't mean I'm deaf."

"What did you say, honey? I'm having a hard time hearing you."

Elyse turns to David in despair.

"Do you see what I have to put up with day in and day out?"

David shakes his head and smiles.

"Don't believe a word of it son. She loves every minute of it. Don't you, sweetie?"

Kenneth goes over to her and tries to kiss her. She playfully moves away.

"Don't you sweetie, me. Come on now, stop your foolishness."

She knows the only thing that will make him do that is to kiss him, so she does.

"There, now, will you sit down and behave yourself, old man."

"Who are you calling old?"

"If the shoe fits…"

David laughs at his in-laws' playfulness.

"You two should have a sit-com. If you only you could hear yourselves."

"She's coming in loud and clear. Trust me."

"Likewise."

David becomes serious all of a sudden.

Both of them ask, "Son, are you all right?"

"I want the two of you to know how much you both mean to me. You've always been there for me no matter what, with love and support. That was something I never got from my parents."

He pauses.

"What is it son," Kenneth asks.

"Well, I know you might not agree with me, but I talked to the doctor this morning and I told him I want to go home."

"But honey…"

"Mom, please just hear me out on this one. Julie has enough with being pregnant without running back and forth several times a day to be here. I want to die at home not here, all hooked up to machines. I want to spend the time I have left with my family, not with doctors and nurses. And I want to go with some dignity."

"Of course, we'll help in any way we can."

"Mom?"

"If this is what you want, I'll support your decision and do whatever I can to help."

"Doctor Robard is going to set things in motion with Hospice so neither of you or Julie has to do anything. I don't want to add any more stress. Just don't tell her though. I want to tell her myself. Okay?"

"Of course," they answer in unison.

David takes a paper from the night table.

"Dad, could you pick these things up for me. I ordered them over the phone, and they're paid for."

"Sure son."

"Thanks, dad, oh, mom, I forgot. Here's the picture of Jocelyn Elyse Taylor."

"Jocelyn Elyse?"

"Yes."

Julie and Nicholas are already back and Nicholas beats his mom to the bed.

"Close your eyes Dad. I have a surprise for you."

David closes his eyes but then opens one as Nicholas gets closer.

"Hey! No peeking."

He puts the package behind his back until he is certain that David has closed both of them again. He stretches his arms out in front of him with the gift in his little hands.

"Okay, you can open them now."

David slowly opens his eyes and looks at the wrapped gift, and then at Nicholas.

"What is it?"

"Open it and see."

David takes the package and slowly pulls it toward him, teasing his son all the time he does so. Then he takes forever to unwrap it. When he does, his eyes get wide as if surprised.

"Wow, a box! This is great. I've always wanted one of these."

Julie and her parents roll their eyes and Nicholas gets restless, as David prolongs the process.

"Daddy, come on. Open the surprise. *Please*."

Everyone else says agrees. "Yes. Please do already."

"Okay, okay, I'm opening it."

Inside the box is a stuffed dog with the banner that says I love you.

"This is the best surprise I've ever had, except for when you were born buddy."

Nicholas, with his eyes wide open in delight, exclaims, "Really?"

"Yes, Nicholas. Julie, can you help my buddy up here so I can hug him?"

"I love you, buddy."

"I love you too daddy."

"That's my big boy. Now tomorrow, I'm going to have a surprise for you."

"What is it?"

"If I told you it wouldn't be a surprise. At least that's what you just told me about my surprise, didn't you?"

"Yes. Dad, how long is tomorrow?"

"Well after you close your eyes tonight and go to sleep, it will seem like just a few minutes until you open them again. Then it will be tomorrow."

"Oh. Okay."

"Now, maybe after one more hug, you can go out to eat with Grandma and Grandpa."

"Oh goody, can we go to the train restaurant?"

"We'll see."

Elyse and Kenneth get up and put their coats on, while Julie helps Nicholas with his coat.

"Aren't you coming Mommy?"

"I think I'll stay here with Daddy and make sure he eats his dinner, especially since he didn't eat his lunch."

She glares at David playfully.

Kenneth looks at David with a smirk.

"And you say your mother and I are funny? Ha!"

Julie looks to David, and then at her father.

"What's that supposed to mean?"

"I'll fill you in on that one later," David answers.

Elyse whispers to Julie, "Do you want us to keep Nicky overnight?"

"You don't mind keeping him, mom?"

"Of course we don't mind."

"Thanks. I call you when I get in."

"Are we ready to go?"

"See you tomorrow, daddy. Bye."

"Bye buddy, I love you."

"I love you too daddy."

"We'll see you tomorrow, son. We love you."

"Love you too."

When they leave, Julie sits on the bed. David leans over and they kiss. Julie runs her hand over his beard.

"You always hated it when I tried to grow a beard didn't you?"

"I don't hate it. It's just that it makes you look older."

"And how is that bad? You obviously don't like the older distinguished type."

"You're right. I like the younger dashing and debonair type of guy."

"Does that mean you'll volunteer to shave it off then?"

"If you're sure you want me too."

"I'm all yours."

"Well, I certainly hope so."

They laugh. Julie goes to fill the plastic basin with water and get the razor, shaving cream, and cologne. Just before she begins, David reaches over to the tape player to put on some of their favorite songs. "My Best Friend' comes on first. When Julie is finished shaving him, she puts on the cologne on the sides of his face. She closes her eyes and drinks in his sensuous smell and expresses how deeply it affects her.

"Judging from your reaction I must be back to my old dashing self again."

"I'd say so. You're very handsome sir. Maybe you'd consider going on a date with me sometime."

"Well I would but what would your husband say?"

"I don't know. Let me ask him."

She leans over, and they kiss.

"Well," David asks.

"He says go for it."

"I was hoping he'd say that."

They laugh and kiss again.

David looks at himself in the small mirror.

"There. Now I'll be all ready for tomorrow."

"Tomorrow, what's tomorrow?"

"Thursday, I think."

"You are so very funny."

"Thank you, I thought so."

"Let me rephrase the question then if you're going to be so technical. What do you have planned for tomorrow that you need to be all handsome-looking? Not that I'm complaining or anything."

"I've got a big date with my wife. However, she doesn't know it yet. I'm going to surprise her."

"Really, well, I promise not to tell her if you let me in on your little secret."

"Do you promise?"

"Scout's honor."

"I don't know if that counts. Were you ever a Girl Scout?"

"Yep, I sold cookies every year."

"Mmm, that sounds good right about now. I love the ones with chocolate, coconut, and caramel."

"I promise to go and try to find some for you when you tell me about this surprise. Now, will you stop changing the subject and tell me?"

"OK, here goes. I'm going home tomorrow and I want to look my best."

Julie jumps off the bed in surprise.

"But I thought. Are you serious, how?"

"Dr. Robard is setting things up with Hospice."

"Hospice, but I…"

David cuts her off mid-sentence.

"Have enough to do. You're running yourself ragged and I'm sure the morning sickness doesn't help any."

Julie sits back down on the edge of the bed and puts her head down. David puts his hand under her chin and lifts her face to caress it.


The next day David comes home with all the needed equipment. He gives Nicholas a train set, Julie a locket, and a music box with a dancing ballerina for Jocelyn, the gifts Kenneth picked up for him.

That afternoon David is sitting by the window, the realization of how much closer the end is now that he is home consumes his thoughts. Julie comes into the room, but he is oblivious to her presence until she puts her hand on his shoulder. He looks up at her and covers her hand with his.

"Glad to be home?"

"Yes."

"Dinner is almost ready."

"Okay."

"I thought maybe after supper we could watch the home movies with Nicholas."

"Sure. That's a good idea, Jules," he says quietly and unconvincingly.

"Are you sure? If you're too tired, we don't have to do it tonight."

"No, tonight's okay. It'll help get me out of this mood.

Okay, well, I'm going to finish dinner. It'll be about another ten minutes.

After dinner, they watch movies of Nicholas as a baby, sledding, riding a pony, and his first swimming lessons. David and Julie spend time alone, looking at pictures of vacations they enjoyed, after Nicholas goes to bed.

The following week Julie is walking by the kitchen when the phone rings. She answers it and only has a short conversation, which isn't audible to David. Julie paces back and forth, wrapping and unwrapping the telephone wire around her hand.

After she hangs up, she takes a deep breath and walks into the den where David is reading. He looks up over the top of his glasses to see her, and motions for her to sit with him on the couch. Instead, Julie sits in the chair some distance from the couch. She has a nervous look on her face, which concerns David.

"Jules, what's the matter? Who was that on the phone and why are you sitting over there?"

"I'm sitting over here in case I have to suddenly leave the room."

"What are you talking about?"

"What I have to say might make you angry with me."

"Jules, what could you have possibly done to make me mad? You're throwing a party and forgot to invite me?"

"I only wish it were that simple."

"Maybe you should tell me."

"I…I wrote letters to your brother and sister."

David takes off his glasses and glares at her. He speaks calmly but firmly, hoping he has misunderstood her.

"You did what?"

"I knew you'd be upset with me at first, but I knew they would never forgive themselves or us if we didn't give them a chance to fix things with you."

"Why do I care how they are going to feel when I'm gone? They never cared while I was alive. So what is going to happen now? Are they going to come and show their pity for me, the loser of the family? How could you, when you know how I feel about them?"

"Because I know that no matter what has come between the three of you, it has been something that has haunted you for a long time. You know you don't want to leave things this way. It's time you made your peace with each other (pauses) for everyone's sake."

"That wasn't your call to make Julie."

"No, you're right, it wasn't. I'm sorry."

Not long after their conversation, David's brother and sister arrive. While Julie is preparing dinner, she can hear intermittent laughter coming from the den. She smiles and wipes a tear from her cheek. She looks down at the vegetables she is dicing.

"Stupid onions," she mutters.

David's brother and sister stay for dinner. They leave with a promise to visit again soon.

After they leave, David asks Julie, "How did you know? I never said anything."

"I just knew. I saw it in your eyes. There was just something else bothering you, something missing that you needed to find. No matter how much you wanted to, you wouldn't have told them. Would you?"

"No, you're right I wouldn't have told them. Thank you."

David takes Julie's face in his hands tenderly kisses her.


Two months pass.

"You've always made everything all right. I could never wait to get home from work to see your smiling face and open arms. The only regret I have is not having more time to spend with you and Nicholas and Jocelyn."

He pauses and licks his chapped lips.

"I don't want to die Jules."

"David, don't. Please. I don't want to think about that right now."

"I'm sorry I didn't mean to get you upset. I said it without thinking."

David pauses, sniffles, and clears his throat.

"So … do you have any regrets about marrying me then, Mrs. Taylor?"

"I have always wanted you from the moment I met you. I must admit you've been complex enough to be confusing at times. But more importantly, you have always been my loving, caring, devoted, strong, sensitive, wonderful man."

She pauses, and then says, "What am I going to do David? I'm losing my best friend."

She sobs and David tries to reassure her through his tears.

"You'll do all right. I'm sure of it."

"But we've done everything together. What about Nicholas and the baby, I don't think I can do this without you."

"Yes, you can."

"How can you be so sure?"

"Because I know you."

One week later Julie is in the den working on a design for a client's website when the hospice nurse comes in to get her.

"Mrs. Taylor?"

"Yes. What is it?"

"You'd better come."

Both women hurry to the bedroom. Julie sits by the bed, taking David's hand in hers.

"David?"

"Jules?"

"I'm right here babe."

"I love you, sweetness," he whispers.

"I love you, David, with all my heart," she answers with tears streaming down her face.

His last breath comes slowly, as he speaks the words that would stay with her always.

"Think of me when you see the sunset, and remember the love I had for you. Please, take care of yourself and the kids for me, Jules."

As they kiss their last tender kiss, Julie feels him slip away. She puts her head down on his chest and sobs.

One month later, Jocelyn is born prematurely, yet the delivery is difficult. By the time the baby arrives, Julie is exhausted. She sleeps until her parents come to visit with Nicholas. The nurse brings Jocelyn in and hands her to Julie. Nicholas caresses his sister's head, as he talks to her.

"Hi, baby. I'm your big brother Nicholas. This is mommy. This is grandma, and this is grandpa. Daddy's not here because mommy says he died and that means we can't see him."

"Mommy?"

"Yes, Nicky?"

"How is the baby going to know about daddy?"

"Well, Nicky, that's part of your job now. You have to help me tell Jocelyn about daddy. That way we won't ever forget him either. We have the pictures and movies we can show her too."

"Oh, yeah, can we show them to her when you come home?"

"We'll see Nicky."

A few days later Julie goes into the kids' rooms to make sure they are both napping. She quietly leaves each of their rooms when she sees they are and goes into her room.

She takes her jeans from the chair and goes to the closet to hang them up. She comes across one of David's shirts with the cologne smell still on it. She puts it to her face and drinks it in. She takes it with her to the bed and still holding it, takes his picture from the nightstand. She caresses his face, and as she places it back on the stand, she notices a cassette tape. Thinking it is the music which David listened to soothe his pain; she places it in the recorder. To her surprise, she hears David's voice instead.

"Jules, you have taken me to places I could never have imagined. In all our years together, I have never once regretted the day we met. You're still the same beautiful girl I fell in love with back then. Don't ever change. Thank you for all your love and support. You were always there for me. You are such a special person. I never understood what you saw in me, but I'm glad you did. Remember the times we had and laugh, don't cry. As you begin to put your life in order, promise me one thing, save a small piece of your heart for me. I know you'll find the strength within you to go on. Know that I love you very much."

After listening to his message, she curls up on the bed with his shirt and cries herself to sleep. An hour passes and the doorbell awakens her. A deliveryman from the florist is at the door with a large white box in his hands.

"Mrs. Taylor?"

"Yes."

"Could you sign here please?"

Julie signs for the package.

"Have a nice day."

"Thank you. You too."

She goes inside, closing the door behind her. She opens the box and finds a dozen long-stemmed roses, along with green ferns and white baby's breath. She finds a vase and carefully places them inside. Putting them on the dining room table, she sits down to read the attached note.

'Sweetness, you're the best thing that ever happened to me. I love you. David'

Julie stares into space, with no strength left to cry anymore. She somehow finds the stamina to get up and make her way to the kitchen. When she does, the receipt falls onto the floor, and she picks it up. Only on examining it does she notice that there isn't a price, but only the order date.

Realizing David had ordered them a few days after he arrived home, a different feeling comes over her, one of renewed strength. Still, she wonders why the flowers arrived on this day. As she looks at the calendar, she notices there is a circle around August 25. Written in the box is, "The day we met."

# The Rainbow's Edge

There had been six months of tension between them; since the time Nicole started working for the company. Her desk was in the front office, so there wasn't much chance of avoiding the daily wisecracks when Dean came in for his work schedule.

He would stand in the path between her desk and the copier until she'd ask him to move out of the way. The one time she offered him a cup of coffee, he made a big deal about it saying sweetly, "Oh, I feel so special."

Not responding, Nicole just rolled her eyes and walked back to her desk. While relating his work stories to anyone who had a listening ear, he would find his way to the candy jar on her desk, at help himself to the contents within, so long as it wasn't candy corn.

The other girls in the office would tolerate his foolishness, but he was starting to get to Nicole. There was something about him that attracted her to him, besides the little cleft in his chin. However, she couldn't quite explain what it was, yet.

He seemed to show interest after two or three months until she responded. Then another side of this complicated man showed through. Was she coming on too strong, or was it his boyhood shyness, which caused him back away? Whatever the reason, it was leaving her confused.

One day a client and Nicole were going over the details of a contact. As he left, he apologized for not catching her first name. Before she could answer, a familiar voice coming from the general direction of the coffee machine, replied "Trouble."

Not missing a beat, Nicole retorted, "No, that's my middle name."

Returning to the previous conversation, she smiled and said "Nicole."

"Thank you for your help, Nicole. Have a great day."

"You have a great day too, Mr. Dawson."

Glancing over, expecting Dean to be surveying the pastry tray, she was surprised instead to see him looking at her. Their eyes met for just a moment, but long enough for them to realize there was something more than just casual teasing between them.

At twenty-eight Dean Andrews was a sales representative for a logging company. Being single, Dean could easily afford to own a house in the woods, and enjoy racing around in his sleek black sports car. He had dated in the past, but his last relationship ended bitterly, leaving him cynical about ever trying again.

As he looked in the mirror, he tried to convince himself that he was content with his single status. His heart told a different story though, which made him question what might happen at the company party that night.

His black double-breasted suit was still in the plastic protection from the cleaners. It hung next to the white shirt on the bedroom door. He sat on the edge of the unkempt bed contemplating whether to go. After all, he didn't dance much. He already paid for his plate, and the boss would certainly have something to say if he didn't show.

"I'll just leave early. I'm sure I can come up with a good excuse by the time the music starts. I hope."

Nicole, on the other hand, was excited about the party, and couldn't wait to get dressed. The velvet ankle-length gown was a shimmering cranberry color. It was straight and caressed her body as she slipped it on. Not wanting to bare her shoulders, she hid them with a short, black velvet jacket. Together with nylons and pumps, she was almost complete. Taking the gold necklace and earrings from her tiny purse, she put them on.

For once, she actually "liked" what she saw. She had her hair and makeup done up professionally at the mall. Unlike her character, she splurged on a new perfume while there was a "perfectly good one" sitting at home on her bureau. A brief thought of Dean made her wonder if she had just imagined that look yesterday, or maybe if she hadn't, he'd ask her to dance tonight.

"What I'm I thinking? He's not interested in me. How could he be? He's just looking for attention, that's all. Who am I trying to kid anyway?" She muttered as she walked away from the mirror. Nevertheless, the tugging of her heartstrings gave her a hopeful feeling.

Everyone seemed to arrive simultaneously. The men headed for the bar while the women headed for the ladies' room. Here, they shared compliments over each other's dresses and hairdos. The men on the other hand shared similar comments of how they thought they'd never arrive on time, due to the time their wives took to get ready.

When everyone sat down, the waiters appeared with soup, salad, and a bottomless breadbasket for each table. When this was finished, they had a delicious surf and turf dinner. The succulent steak and the shrimp; battered just right, were complemented by a steaming hot baked potato. If that hadn't been enough, or even if it had, the chocolate cake finished the meal off nicely. Would they even be able to rise from the chairs to dance? Maybe a little more time conversing would help.

It didn't take Nicole long to get up and dance. She loved to dance and it showed. Dean watched her from a distance. She was having so much fun she didn't even notice. After quite a few fast songs in a row, the lights dimmed and a slow song began. Getting off the dance floor, Nicole stood with some of the other employees who were "sitting" this one out. Dean walked up from behind her and held his hand out to her. Somehow, he nervously managed one word.

"Dance?"

Startled and equally as nervous, Nicole placed her slender fingers into his stalwart hand. He led her back to the dance floor and turned to face her. Her subtle perfume awakened his senses and made her more captivating. At first, she couldn't lift her eyes to meet his. When she did, his smile made her blush. Although they were dancing together, the space between them made it awkward. With her heart racing faster she thought, "He must be able to feel how uneasy I am." Little did she know that he was feeling the same way.

As the music faded, she thought she'd escape to the ladies' room to recover. They thanked one another for the dance. However, before she made her exit, he asked if he could buy her a drink. Clearing her throat, she agreed to a White Zinfandel and excused herself, promising to return.

He was already sitting at her table when she got there. After they conversed for a few minutes they began to feel more at ease with one another, and a comfortable sensation draped over them.

As the band began to play 'Unchained Melody', Nicole broke the conversation with "Oh, I love this song!"

Dean's eyes lit up. "Let's dance to it then."

Dancing slightly closer than they did before, the sweet attraction replaced the nervousness. Everyone briefly interrupted his or her conversations to see what was going on here. They were happy for them.

The clock showed the hours passing, but it went unnoticed by their newly found friends. The party ended much too soon, everyone saying their good-byes. Neither Dean nor Nicole wanted to leave. Dean felt compelled to ask her to go to breakfast.

"We just ate not long ago. I'm not hungry."

Seeing the disappointment in his eyes she said, "Well I might be able to handle a coffee and Danish."

Jumping up he blurted, "Great, I'll get our coats."

He began to run off, but came to a sudden halt, realizing he didn't have the ticket for Nicole's coat. He slowly turned around bearing a silly grin. Nicole laughed and then flashed a tantalizing smile, which made him melt.

"Do you want me to go with you?"

"That would be a good idea."

They had all they could do to keep their composure while the attendant searched for their coats.

"Have a safe drive home. The snow's been coming down for about an hour now."

The first snow was perfect. They stood outside looking up at the delicate lace. Nicole's eyelashes caught them as they descended upon her face.

"I just love the snow, don't you?"

When no answer came, she turned. Dean was staring at her with a dreamy look in his eyes. He noticed that she caught him, and the blood pounded in his ears. He shyly looked away.

"Hmm, yes, I do. I love to ski. Do you ski?"

"No, but I'd like to learn."

"Maybe we could go sometime."

"I'd like that. When is usually the best time?"

"I've found that the best time is in the winter."

"You're hilarious."

It was surprisingly warm without the wind.

"There's an all-night diner down the street from here. The cars will be safe here if you feel like walking."

"That would be nice."

"So Nicole, did you always live here in Maine?"

"No, I grew up in Virginia with my sisters and brother."

"Are they all still there?"

"My brother still lives there. One of my sisters lives on Long Island, and the other one lives in North Dakota with her husband."

"And where do your parents live?"

"My father died when I was seventeen, just three days before my high school graduation, and my mother passed away last April."

"Oh, I'm sorry."

"Thank you. What about you?"

"Well, I grew up in San Diego with my parents and my brother. They got divorced when we were young and my mother brought us here. She got remarried and my brother eventually moved back with my father."

The server wandered over to their booth.

"Are you ready to order?"

"I'll have a coffee and an apple Danish, grilled, please."

"And you sir?"

"I'll have the same, thank you."

"So, what do you do for entertainment, besides skiing, Dean?"

"I enjoy hiking. I also carry a camera with me at all times because I love photography."

"I like taking pictures too, but I hate being in them."

"That's unfortunate."

"Why?"

"Because I'd like to get a picture of the way you look tonight."

"Thank you for the compliment but I despise having my picture taken."

"Why?"

"Because I don't like the way I look in person, never mind making it more permanent with a photograph. Anyway..."

"Do you have any hobbies... other than avoiding photographs?"

"Yes. I love dancing and horseback riding, not at the same time of course. Oh and I love to cook, especially Italian food."

"Italian, that's my weakness."

"Well, maybe we could have dinner sometime. I make amazing lasagna with homemade garlic bread."

"Stop it, you're making me hungry."

"Then it's a good thing the waitress is coming with our food."

They have their midnight snack at 2 a.m. and exchange stories, interests, and plans, from his wanting to go to Texas in the spring, to her dream of traveling to Tuscany someday. By six, they had enough caffeine to keep them going all day, which didn't sound like a bad idea. Walking back to their cars, they discovered they only lived about twelve miles from one another.

"I'll follow you so I know where your house is, and then I'll go home and change and meet you back there at nine. Is that all right with you?"

"Great. That'll give me enough time to freshen up and change."

Nicole couldn't wait to get home so she could run through the house with excitement. She was ready to burst by the time they reached her street. She went to Dean's car, confirmed their plans, and then watched him speed away.

Once inside she took off her shoes, slid across the floor and spun around. She headed for the shower, but stopped short to look in the bedroom mirror.

"I'm glowing," she whispered. "I can't believe this is happening. Oh no, what am I going to wear?"

Ransacking her drawers and closet, she finally found the needed attire to make a rather attractive outfit that would be appropriate for wherever they were going.

The warm shower helped to calm her nerves. By the time she finished getting dressed and fixing her hair, it was 8:00.

"Good, that will give me a little time to straighten up around here."

Dean drove home with the oldies blasting from the speakers. It seemed that every song reminded him of Nicole. He felt like a new man, as he ran across the lawn to the front door. Finding the right key was never a problem, until now. He fumbled and the door flew open.

"Woo hoo," he shouted, taking the stairs two at a time.

He quickly jumped in the shower. While drying his hair, he glanced at the medicine chest over the sink. He didn't recognize his reflection. It wasn't the same one as the night before.

"What is this woman doing to me? I can't remember ever feeling like this before. I've only been away from her for fifteen minutes and already it's driving me crazy."

After getting dressed, he grabbed his coat, wallet, and camera, and headed out, stopping at the florist buy a single, white rose. The day would certainly be one to remember.

Nicole had just finished cleaning when the doorbell rang. She took a deep breath and walked over to answer it, taking her coat from the hook. Dean handed her the rose.

"Are you ready?"

"Thank you, yes, I am."

"Then let's go."

"So where do you want to go?"

"I hadn't stopped to think about where we were going. I just got ready."

"Me too, hmm, let's see, how about a movie?"

"You want to watch a movie, at nine in the morning?"

"Well, I would hate for you to think that all I do is eat, but it has been a while since we had the Danish."

"My stomach is starting to feel empty, now that you mention it."

"How does the House of Pancakes sound?"

During breakfast, a new blanket of snow replaced the one that had melted in the morning sun. A walk in the park, to rid of some of the calories consumed, proved fun. It seemed harmless enough, just walking to the gazebo until Nicole decided to throw a "little" snowball at an unsuspecting Dean. This of course started an all-out war.

White powder flew everywhere, as they tried to see who could make and throw them the fastest. When they were finally exhausted from this, they collapsed on the ground laughing. Then another favorite pastime began to take shape, snow angels.

Standing to examine them, Dean proclaimed, "Look at the difference. Mine is a rather BIG snow angel. It looks like it needs to lose a few pounds. Don't you think?"

Nicole giggled. "No. Haven't you seen an angel with muscles before?"

"No, I haven't. And even if it did have muscles, they would be where you claim these have appeared."

Throwing one last snowball, Nicole made a run for the car with Dean at her heels. She almost reached it, when a sudden breeze took her beret. Her long black hair fell over her shoulders and across her face. Dean had retrieved the beret quickly enough to be by her side before she could react. With the hat in one hand, he reached over and gently pushed aside her hair to reveal her green eyes.

As she started to speak, he put his finger to her lips. Placing his hand behind her head, he brought her to him and tenderly kissed her. She responded to him as her body trembled under his touch.

"Do you know how beautiful you are Nicole?" he whispered.

She shook her head.

"Well, it's about time someone told you."

He took her chin in his hand.

"Look at me."

She raised her eyes to meet his.

"You are beautiful whether you want to believe it or not."

"Dean, I'd love to believe that it was even a little true. However, I've been through some things in my life that make me think otherwise.

And especially where I'm not very good at taking compliments, it might take some getting used to."

"Well then, I guess I'll just have to be patient, but I'm not giving up trying to convince you.

"Come on. It's getting too windy out here. We need to warm up."

While waiting for the car to heat up, the discussed the dilemma of where to go next.

"Do you want to go to the mall? I need to get some equipment for the ski trip."

"Sure."

"Speaking of ski trips..."

He takes a paper with the information out of his coat pocket and hands it to her.

"Interested in joining me?"

"The weekend of February 20th, I'll have to let you know. It sounds like a good idea on paper, but I don't know about me on skis."

"You'll get the hang of it in no time, I bet. I'll show you how."

"I didn't know you were a ski instructor too," she laughed.

"There's a lot about me you don't know, but if you stick around you'll find out."

Three hours, and six shopping bags later, they were left tired of being on their feet.

"I don't think I can walk another inch."

"No offense Nicole, but I'm just a little too tired to carry you to the car."

"That's too bad."

"I want to thank you for today, Dean. I haven't had fun like this in a long time."

"Me either. You know sometimes when you get hurt, you find it hard to trust someone enough to let them get close to you."

"I know what you mean. No matter how long it's been, when the next person comes along, the defenses automatically go up. Then if you're still in the hurting or bitter stages, you tend to take it out on them. The only major relationship I had lasted nine years before it ended five years ago. The emotional scars took a long time to heal. He did a lot of damage. Sometimes a situation will come up and I find myself looking at things in his perspective instead of mine.

Then I react or say some-thing as if he was still here. After that, I beat myself up mentally for letting him get to me, even now."

"It's only natural that you would do that if you haven't had anyone treat you differently since then."

"I never thought about it that way before. You're right. That makes so much sense. What about you?"

"It was about two years ago when the relationship I was in turned sour."

"What happened?"

"The girl I was with just dropped me out of nowhere. She gave me some lame excuse, but I think there was someone else. I was devastated. I thought everything was going well up until that point. Guess I was wrong.

"Anyway, depression set in and I was a mess until a good friend of mine snapped me out of it. He convinced me that I had to get on with my life. I started doing more things but I certainly didn't want another relationship at that point. I pushed away anyone who tried to make me feel emotions that I didn't want to feel. Of course, then I looked like a jerk, but I couldn't help it. I just wasn't ready."

"And now," Nicole tenderly questioned.

"Truthfully," Dean paused. "It might be sound crazy, but, and forgive me Nicole if I'm out of line. The last six months have been so different for me. I've never wanted to be with anyone more than I want to be with you."

Dean looked up to see Nicole crying. Going over to her he asks, "Nicole? What's wrong? I am way out of line. I knew it. It's only been two days and I'm throwing all this at you. I'm sorry, I..."

"Dean, please don't be sorry. Even though it's been such a short time, I've been feeling the same way. I was confused at first especially when you seemed interested until I reacted. Now I know why you retreated into the safety zone."

"Nicole, you don't know how much it was killing me to do that. I just was so afraid of being torn apart again, even though I didn't think you were the kind of person who would or even could do that."

"Then why did you call me 'trouble'?"

"It was because right from the beginning you went straight to my heart. I could feel you breaking down the walls that I had put up, and I couldn't do anything to stop it. I didn't think I could love again or that anyone could love me. Then as time went on, I knew it was a losing battle, but one I will never regret losing."

The months of tension and sheer nervousness between them had worked to turn them into more than just friends virtually overnight.

The next eight months seemed like a whirlwind of events. A simple office friendship blossomed into a flourishing relationship. A marriage of two people who deserved to love, and be loved had found one another amidst all the adversity and heartache in their lives. In a world saturated with loneliness and disappointment, true love can and will prevail for those who are willing to seek and patiently wait for it; remembering that anything of great worth is worth waiting for.

## The Music

Dana had finally finished correcting all the term papers and decided to go to the coffee shop. It was such a popular spot though, that sometimes there weren't any empty seats found on either of the two levels. Her favorite place to sit was in one of several booths, in particular, the last ones in the back, facing the small fireplace in the corner. Next to this, there were two loveseats, a couch, and a bookshelf with plenty of well-read books.

Dana spread out her papers and reference books on the table, leaving little room for her mocha cappuccino. She found it easy to unwind if she wrote. Sometimes it was poetry, but most of the time it was short stories. The coffee shop setting allowed her to study people to get ideas for her characters.

Patrick often frequented the shop, just to sit and read. Unlike Dana, he drank decaffeinated coffee after seven; otherwise, he would be awake all night. On this particular night, there was only one seat available, a small table located next to Dana's booth. Smiling politely, he pulled out his chair, sat down, and began to immerse himself in the day's news.

Dana had reciprocated the smile and returned to her story. Perusing the room, as she so often did when writer's block set in, she saw a young woman on the couch, laughing heartily. Then, her eyes caught Patrick's profile. Discreetly she studied him - short wavy blond hair, long sideburns (which she didn't like), the clef in his chin (which she did like), and he was well built.

"Hmm, no wedding ring," she thought. "He's either not married, or he's hiding something. I wonder how old he is. He doesn't look much older than thirty-three or thirty-four."

As she glanced up at his face, he caught her and smiled with one uplifted eyebrow. She nervously smiled and looked back at her story, cautiously looking over every so often. Getting away with it twice, she chanced a third time. This was pushing it. He caught her again! This time she dropped her head to the table in sheer embarrassment. Looking up, she apologized for staring.

"No need to apologize. I'm flattered. Surprised, but flattered. We should properly introduce ourselves. Patrick Lewis."

"Dana Bradshaw."

"Well, now that the formalities are over, would you mind if I joined you? If you have enough room over there that is."

"Of course, just let me straighten out this mess of papers."

When he stood, she figured he was about 5'9.

"There, all cleaned up. Well, sort of."

"Correcting papers?"

"No, actually I've already done that today. This is just my scribbling."

"So you do correct papers. You're a teacher, I presume?"

"Yes, English literature at the university."

A smile came across his face and he snapped his fingers.

"I knew I've seen you somewhere other than here, before."

"Are you a student at the university," she asked.

"Hardly, I teach Anthropology."

"That sounds interesting."

Sipping the last drop of her coffee, Dana looked disappointed.

"Can I get you another coffee?"

"Hmm, oh yes, that would be great. I need the caffeine, you know, to get the creativeness going."

She reached for her purse.

"I've got it. What are you drinking, espresso?"

"No, no, it's just regular coffee. Espresso's a little too much caffeine, especially for this size cup."

"I'll be right back."

It took about ten minutes, with the long line. It seemed crowded for a Thursday night. Then again, the drama club was there after the dress rehearsal.

"Here you go."

"Thank you."

"If you don't mind me asking, do you write poetry?"

"I write short stories; although I have written a few poems in my day."

"In your day...you make it sound like you're seventy years old. Now I know you can't be over thirty, but then it isn't polite to ask a woman her age. So I won't ask."

"Well thank you for the compliment, but I don't mind telling, since I plan to grow old gracefully. I'll be thirty-five next month."

"I don't believe it."

"Well I could show you my driver's license to prove it, but I'm not very photogenic."

"No, I'll take your word for it, your age not your picture. Never doubt a lady, I've always said."

"Those are words to live by."

"So how old do you think I am. Be kind now," he chuckled.

"I was wondering that, as you were sitting at the table."

"You mean when you were spying on me?"

"I wasn't spying, just looking."

"And what conclusion did you come to?"

"I'd say thirty-three, thirty-four."

"I said to be kind, not ludicrous," he laughed.

"I'm serious."

"Well, now I have a friend for life. Could you please tell that to my mirror? It keeps reminding me that I'm going to be forty-one in July. Plus I have a driver's license to prove it."

"Touché."

The small talk went on for about another forty-five minutes, before Patrick had to leave.

"I am sorry that I have to leave, but I have an early engagement in the morning. Hopefully, we can do this again soon."

"I would enjoy your company again Patrick. I'm usually here on Tuesdays and Thursdays. Then again we are both employed at the same place."

"Maybe we can compare our schedules and have lunch?"

"I like that very much. Here is my extension number at school."

"It has been a pleasure, Miss Bradshaw. I will call you when we return next week. Good night."

"Good night and thank you again for the coffee."

Instead of calling the following week, Patrick found her classroom at the university and presented her with flowers. They went to lunch twice that week. The following Friday night they met at the university lounge, after Patrick's mandatory meeting that his department head had called at the last minute.

"I made some cherry cheesecake and brought it along. Did you want coffee or tea?"

"I'll have tea, please. Yum, cheesecake is one of my weaknesses, how did you know?"

"It was just a guess. It's one of my weaknesses too."

"Delicious, just the way I like it. So, did you have more papers to correct tonight?"

"No, thank goodness, but that won't last for long."

"I hear you loud and clear. You must have time for your writing then?"

"No, I had some reading to catch up on instead. Do you use cream and or sugar?"

"Two sugars please."

"There, this should warm you up a little. It's colder than usual tonight."

Looking down at the case he had brought in with him, Dana asked, "musically talented too?"

"Excuse me? Oh this, well I'd like to think maybe a little."

He placed his mug on the coaster and picked up the case. Opening it, he revealed a handsome looking flute.

"I play when I want to relax mostly. It helps me to unwind. Would you like me to play?"

"Finish your tea first. I can wait."

He finished his drink and removed the flute from the case. Pursing his lips, he gently placed them upon it. Almost immediately, Dana was entranced. She watched the way his hands gracefully held it. She closed her eyes and concentrated. She could hear his every breath as the melody flowed through her. He ended before she realized it.

"Dana?"

His voice startled her, bringing her back to reality.

"Yes? Oh, I'm sorry. It was beautiful."

"You seemed to be elsewhere."

"Yes."

"Where did it take you?"

"Somewhere I've never been before. It was a tranquil place. I felt like I belonged there."

"I'm glad the music had such an effect on you. Now it's your turn."

"But I don't know how to play the flute."

Patrick laughed. "No, but you do have some stories or poetry that you've written. Care to share them with me?"

"Well..."

"Come on now. I'm interested to see what you write about, as I'm guessing you have a wild imagination."

"What makes you say that?"

"Oh, I don't know," he smiled. "It was just a guess."

Dana went to retrieve some of her poems. She handed him one called 'Autumn Fires' and placed the rest on the table.

"Care for another cup of tea?"

"Yes, that would be nice."

She left their cups on the counter, and excused herself to the bathroom.

While she was away, he read 'Autumn Fires'. Placing it down on the table, he noticed one entitled 'Lovers' Journey'. Intrigued, he read that one too.

Just as he finished, he heard Dana's footsteps, and put it back under the one she had given him. This one he kept firmly fixed in his mind for further reference.

"So what did you think of it?"

"You certainly have a knack for capturing the essence of nature. It was so vivid. I enjoyed it very much."

"I'm glad."

They looked at each other for a moment without saying a word.

"So, do you have any other poems," he asked reaching over to them.

"I think there's a few there. Let me see."

She shuffled past 'Lovers' Journey' and kept looking.

"What's wrong with the last one?"

"It's not one of my better ones," she said without looking up.

He smiled to himself, knowing which one she skipped.

"Here, this one's all right."

"Hmm, 'Vermont Mist'."

After reading it he said, "Do you miss living in the country?"

"Yes, I do."

"Would you ever move back?"

"Maybe someday I will, but for now I can be content to live here."

"Are you content?"

Dana looked away and didn't answer.

"I'm sorry. That was too personal. I didn't mean to pry."

"I thought moving here, away from memories, would help. I guess to some extent it has, but I wouldn't say I'm content, no."

"It seems like we all have something that haunts us from time to time, something or someone we're running away from. Somewhere along the line, we need to put them behind us, and move on. Otherwise, we let them run our lives forever."

That night became a starting point for their budding romance. They met every morning, stopped for a coffee, and went to work. When their schedules allowed for it, they had lunch together. There were many candlelight dinners and moonlit walks. Now, visits to the theater and museums, replaced the loneliness.

One night at the university, Patrick asked Dana's opinion of a new melody he had written. Seeing how transfixed she was when he finished playing, he knew he had reached her heart.

"I've never heard anything so beautiful. It's even more wonderful than the first song you played for me."

"That's because I didn't have you as the inspiration for the first one."

"Oh, Patrick," she blushed.

"I have a confession to make Dana."

"What is it?"

"Remember that night, when I read some of your poetry?"

"Yes."

"Well...when you were out of the room, I came across your poem, 'Lovers' Journey', and read it. I knew that I could write a melody for it, but it wasn't until we started spending time together, that I realized how much it meant to me...how much you mean to me. Being with you has changed my whole life."

"I feel the same way. All my life I've only wanted one thing, someone I could tell my innermost thoughts to, someone who shared my passion for life and understood my heart and feelings; a soul mate. After a while though, I'd convinced myself that this ideal person would only exist for someone else. I even kept a journal that I've never let anyone read."

"Can I be so bold as to ask if you trust me enough to read it? I have seen so much of your love for life in the short time we have spent together. Your heart is an open book. You hold nothing back when it comes to your thoughts, feelings, and memories. You are a woman of strong convictions, and I admire you for that quality. I would only read what you have carefully penned to know you better. It is something I can and will respect, as I respect you, if you feel that your journal should remain personal."

"At one time I felt it was something I would never share with anyone. This journal reveals so much of me that sometimes when I stop, and reread what I wrote; it scares me to think that I felt that way. Nevertheless, I do trust you not to take those thoughts and make fun of them or make light of them in any way. I have come to see what a good, honest man you are Patrick, kind and compassionate. Please read it with an open heart and mind.

She handed the journal to him, knowing that at this very moment she would relinquish to him every emotion, feeling, thought, hope, and dream that captured the essence of her very existence. She was now going to reveal what made her who she was as a person. If he betrayed her, she would never be able to confide in the blank white canvas, which awaited the soft stroke of her loving fingers, as she painted the pictures through words...the words of the deepest innermost parts of her soul. Once he began the journey into her soul, there was no turning back.

Journey into the Soul

Your love filled the void I've held within me for so long

I used to stay awake at nights with a gnawing feeling of emptiness

Longed for the warmth of your loving arms embracing me

I watched movies where the characters convince you into believing that they are deeply in love, just by how they gaze into one another eyes, how he runs after her when he thinks he's lost her, and she appears before him with a forgiving heart.

I wanted to experience such an undying love and deep-rooted desire which I thought would never be fulfilled, but instead, linger within me; constantly nagging at me; my spirit and strength fighting against it, so as not to concede to dark despair.

I continued to watch those movies and listen to romantic music, even though they would tear me apart inside. I only did this so that I would not become cynical and banish all thoughts of ever being loved, and cherished by someone whom I could trust to hold my inner thoughts and dreams close to his hear; a man whom I could give myself to, forever!

There were times when I gave in and lost the hope - abandoned the dream, the one thing I always wanted my entire life.

He puts his fingers to my lips and gently brushes against them.

My heart begins to beat rapidly.

I stand frozen in time. Our eyes meet and a smile brightens his face.

If only we had forever and not just this moment to be captured in love's tender bonds.

The feeling that envelopes my entire being is the warmth he radiates and the trueness of his unending loyalty.

His eyes sparkle as he playfully teases.

Still, without uttering a word, he leans toward me and reaches out to embrace me...

I am snatched away - back to reality! Its harshness forces me to fight against it, trying desperately to catch my breath!

"PLEASE, LET ME RETURN! DON'T TAKE ME AWAY FROM HIM!"

The chasm between us rips open and this time it is wider and deeper than before. It crushes me to the point where a torrent river of tears flows and suppresses my voice.

When will it be my turn? Or rather will it ever be? Am I ever to taste love's exquisite honey? Will it be able to quench the burning which resides deep within and bubbles forth at times unannounced?

Chills flood my entire being!

I want to find the one who will love me unconditionally, to hear him whisper my name, to have his strong arms hold me as I gaze upward, only to be lost in his eyes.

It is said, "the greatest beauty on earth is found in the hearts of those who love."'


Dana tried not to stare at Patrick as he silently read. He finished, carefully closed it, and ran his hand across the cover. Finally looking up at her, without saying a word, he motioned for her to come and sit beside him. She went, and after she sat down, he took her face in his hands, and tenderly kissed her lips.

He drew back and whispered," I have never, in all the years that I have been on this earth, ever read anything so expressive and heart wrenching. I consider myself privileged to have been able to share an important part of who you are and I can only hope that you come to find the answer to your dreams. You deserve all the happiness this world can offer you, Dana. I would someday like to know that your dreams were fulfilled."

"Patrick, I left out what I hope will be the ending of this chapter. Without being too presumptuous, I would like to add a final sentence before closing this part of my life.

'Now I know I've found the only person who could ever fulfill these dreams and who I would like to begin a new chapter of my life with...Patrick Lewis'

Patrick took her in his arms and whispered, "I have found the woman I want to spend the rest of my life with too."

They shared their first passionate kiss since they had met. This pivotal moment in their relationship did not last for more than a moment though.

As they sat on the couch, immersed in each other, the unexpected screeching of the fire alarm in the hall jolted them back to reality. Jumping up off the couch Patrick grabbed Dana's hand as they ran for the door. Forgetting to feel it first before opening it, a rush of air came in at them. Everyone was running down the hall to the exit. The smoke made it difficult to see their way clearly.

Making it to the stairwell, they tried, along with everyone else to make their descent to safety. As they were approaching the second-floor landing, an anxious woman pushed past Dana. Her hand slipped from Patrick's grasp. Losing her footing, she plummeted to the landing below, hitting her back against the wall. Some took note of this and slowed down, but others were more concerned for their own survival and continued on.

Patrick frantically made his way through the crowd. Dana was trying to speak when he reached her, but she couldn't catch her breath. He wanted to carry her, but he was afraid of doing further damage by moving her.

"Someone, please call the paramedics," he shouted.

"Don't try to move Dana, help will be here soon."

Tears filled her eyes as the excruciating pain shot through her back and down her legs.

They could hear the sounds of the fire crew below them. The alarms and sirens made the situation worse. After what seemed hours, the paramedics reached them, and carried her on a stretcher to the waiting ambulance. After some deliberation, they let Patrick ride with her, but in the front of the rig, so that they could have room to work. Through the window, he could see them put the oxygen mask on her. She closed her eyes, and he found himself trying to catch his own breath. Seeing the anxiety on his face, the E.M.T. gave him a thumbs-up sign to reassure him that she was just resting now that she could breathe a little easier.

At the hospital, they wheeled Dana into the emergency trauma room and shut the doors behind them, leaving Patrick to see her only through the glass, again. The orderly came out and asked him to go to the admitting desk.

"How is she?"

"She's stable, but we need to take x-rays to see how much damage there is."

"Can I see her," Patrick asked desperately.

"Right now we need you to go to the desk and fill out the needed information, so we can treat her."

Obediently, Patrick made his way to the desk. His head was spinning. The questions the triage nurse was asking seemed jumbled, and he was becoming increasingly impatient. He answered her to the best of his ability, given the circumstances. As soon as she finished, he asked for directions to the x-ray department. He couldn't sit still.

He began to pace the floor, and then he saw the orderly from the trauma room run by. Before he could get to the doorway, they rushed Dana past him and into another room. He slipped in through the door before it shut.

"Dana? What's happening?"

"Sir, you'll have to wait outside."

"Can't someone at least tell me what is going on?"

One of the nurses walked away from the gurney, and escorted him outside the room.

"Sir, your wife went into a coma while we were finishing the x-rays."

It was as if someone punched Patrick in the stomach. He doubled over.

"What, a coma?"

"We're doing everything we can to help her. But she needs surgery."

Another blow, this one struck him harder and he felt as if he would vomit. He grabbed the nearest chair and fell into it, putting his head between his knees.

"I don't understand. What made her go into the coma in the first place?"

"It appears from the x-rays that she has a herniated disc in her neck, which is pressing on her spinal cord. As soon as we can get her stabilized, we're taking her to the operating room."

"Can I see her before you do that?"

With the pain still in his gut, he followed the nurse back into the room. However, he didn't have time to prepare himself for what he saw.

Dana was gray and swollen. There seemed to be countless tubes and wires attached to her lifeless body. There were machines and monitors all around her. He walked up to her side and carefully touched her face. Without lifting her hand, he put his over it and leaned over to her. With tear-filled eyes and a lump in his throat he whispered, "I love you, Dana. Please don't leave me."

"Sir, you'll have to leave now. We're ready to take her into surgery."

As his tears fell upon her face, he kissed her forehead.

"I'll be waiting right here for you, my love."

"I'll show you where the waiting room is upstairs. The doctor will come out and let you know how your wife's operation went when they're finished."

"Wife" that word stood out repeatedly in his mind. He ran his fingers anxiously through his hair as he contemplated the thought of whether Dana would ever be able to become his wife now.

Then the thoughts changed, to Dana's mother. I should call and let her know, he thought to himself. He tried hard to remember where in Vermont she lived. Brattleboro? No, Bennington. He found the payphones and called information. Receiving the number, he made the dreaded call.

Irene Bradshaw answered after the first ring, and with an unsteady voice, he spoke.

"Mrs. Bradshaw?"

"This is she."

"This is Patrick Lewis, one of Dana's colleagues."

"Yes, Dana's mentioned you before. What can I do for you?"

"Well, um..."

His voice cracked and Irene sensed the desperation.

"Patrick, what's wrong with Dana?"

"She had an accident tonight and she's in the hospital."

"Is she all right? What happened?"

Her voice now shared the desperation, coupled with anxiety.

"There was a fire in one of the university buildings."

"Oh God, no!"

"We were almost down the stairs when...she was knocked down to the next landing."

"Oh, God," she repeated.

"She's in surgery now for a herniated disc in her neck..."

"But?"

"I'm sorry. She went into a coma before they brought her to the operating room."

A loud, painful scream came over the receiver, and Patrick reeled back.

"Mrs. Bradshaw?"

"I'll be there as soon as possible. Which hospital is she in?"

"It's the New York University Hospital. Please get someone to drive you, for your safety."

"Yes, I will. Thank you."


The two-hour drive seemed like ten, but they arrived safely. They met, and Patrick explained what the doctor had told him.

"The surgery was a success, but Dana is still in a coma because of the swelling. They're monitoring her, but for now, we just have to wait and pray."

"Can we see her?"

"Of course, I'll take you to her room."

Irene was not prepared to see her daughter this way.

"I can't believe it, my Dana."

Patrick slid the chair over to the bed and urged her to sit down.

"I'll leave you with her. Can I get you anything?"

"A glass of water, please. I need to take my heart medicine."

It had been three weeks since the accident, and Dana still had not regained consciousness. Her mother stayed at Dana's apartment at night, and her days at the hospital. It was taking its toll on her. The doctors became concerned and began to keep a close eye on her.

Patrick unfortunately spent his days at the university, after the first week. He hated it. He couldn't concentrate, and both the faculty and students felt it. He knew he had to try to keep himself going, although the nights spent by her side were taxing him.

By the end of the third week, the doctors painfully asked them to consider whether to keep her on life-support. Being more than Irene could take, she suffered a minor heart attack, only hours after they suggested it.

Up to this point, she kept Dana's brother, Daniel, updated via long-distance. Now, with this new development, he flew in from Arizona, and Patrick met him at the airport.

Everyone, including the doctors, agreed that the decision could wait until Irene had recuperated sufficiently. It was a difficult decision to make under "normal" circumstances, let alone now.

Then, a week later, Dana took the burden from their shoulders.

It was a Wednesday night, about seven-thirty. Patrick had just arrived; relieving Daniel, so he could go to the apartment and rest. His spent his energy too, and he needed to talk with his wife and kids.

Patrick had talked to Dana night after night. This evening, however, he wanted to try something different. He closed the door behind him and sat by the bed. He then reached under his chair for the little black case. He wondered why he hadn't thought of it before. He opened it, removed the flute, and slowly placed it against his lips. As hard as it was for him, he played a melody, which if it had words, would have sounded something like this:

Dana, I love you, and I always will

You showed me the passion of your soul, your beauty; both inner and outer which you possess

Your love of nature, and the way you find delight in the simpler things in life

You asked for nothing materially, only for me to share the sunset and sunrise with you, the mountain-view, the first snow, the first autumn leaves, falling downward, so gracefully from above

We walked the beach at night and danced under the stars

With each of these, you expressed the type of excitement someone else would show only if they received the entire world on a silver platter

When I am down or have an exhausting day, your smile and laughter refreshes me

You light up a dark room when you grace it with your presence

I hear your voice on the phone at night before I go to sleep, and I pray that my dreams of you and me running free, together, forever become a reality

My life is incomplete without you and I want you to be there when I awake in the morning, and when I close my eyes in the evening

I no longer want to go through this life alone, for without you I merely exist, and I want to live and experience the passion for life that you hold within you...

I love you my Irish rose

As he finished, the lump in his throat made him put his head on his arms, which were leaning on the bed rail, and sob. The tears racked his body, but he could not stop. As if lightning had struck him, he jolted, feeling something softly brush against his arm. Thinking he was surely imagining this, he looked at Dana through tear-soaked eyes.

"Dana! Oh God, thank you!"

Without any hesitation, he found the nurses' call button by the bed and pushed it hard. Within seconds, there was a nurse by his side. A few minutes later two doctors came in. Seeing the fear in her eyes, they explained what had happened and how they were going to proceed from there.

After a thorough examination, they determined that Dana could hold her own, without the extra support from the machines. As they took the tube from her throat, she gasped for air. In seconds, she took the deepest breath she had ever taken. Her lungs filled, her breathing steadied, and she began to calm down. Her voice was just a whisper as she called Patrick's name.

"I'm right here Dana."

"I heard you playing, but I couldn't find you."

"But you did find me. Please don't ever leave me again."

"I won't, I promise. I'll always stay with you."

She half-closed her eyes and licked her chapped lips. Patrick trembled and fought to catch his breath.

"We'll keep her monitored for now," the doctor assured him.

"I'll send someone for her mother and brother."

"Thank you, thank you for everything doctor."

The doctor saw the flute lying on the chair and motioned to Patrick.

"I think the thanks goes to you in this instance, son."

Patrick glanced over at the flute and knew its music had brought his Irish rose back to him.

## Primary Image

"Let's go, hustle, hustle. I want to see some defense out there. We have a big game tomorrow. Jackson, come here son. You look winded. Did you take your inhaler before we started," he asked with a fatherly smile.

Henry looked down at his sneakers and shook his head negatively.

"And why not," the coach inquired, hoping for a verbal answer.

"My mom couldn't afford it again coach. You know how it is," he replied, looking up into the coach's understanding eyes.

"Okay, after the game we'll stop by the pharmacy and see if we can't get you that inhaler. All right guys take five and get some water."

"Thanks, coach."

On the way home, Ty paid for the medicine, and bought a doll for a special little girl, before walking Henry home. Henry's mother thanked him repeatedly. She also made sure he took some of her homemade soup, as a token of her appreciation. He hoped the jar would withstand the ride on the train so that he could enjoy its contents when he arrived home.

Quietly, he opened the door to his modest apartment, and barely placed the two items on the kitchen table when an excited little girl came running from her room. She squealed with delight and jumped into Ty's waiting arms.

"How is my big girl today? I've missed you so much."

Carefully holding her with one arm, he took the doll off the table and handed it to her.

Another squeal, louder this time, issued forth.

"Papa, she's beautiful. Thank you. Can I go and play with her?"

"Yes, but only after I get a kiss from you."

She kissed him, and then as soon as her feet touched the floor again, she ran into her room to play. Ty watched her, and listened as she introduced the new doll to all of the old ones. As he was in a trance-like state, he didn't notice that his sister had walked into the room.

"Another doll Ty, she's going to need a room just for them pretty soon."

"Hmm, I'm sorry Denise. What did you say?"

"Nothing, it doesn't matter anyway because you're not going to stop buying them for her. What's this," she asked referring to the jar of soup.

"It's soup, from Henry's mother. She wanted to thank me."

"What did she want to thank you for? Not that it's any of my business."

"Oh, for helping him out with his game," he said as he found a microwavable bowl to put the soup in.

"Uh-huh, just for helping him with his game?"

"Yeah, why do you ask?"

"Ty, you forget that I've been here for two years now, and I see what's happening. Did you buy that boy his medicine again," she asked with her hands positioned on her hips.

"You look like momma you know. Are you going to swat me with that dishtowel on your shoulder too," he laughed, while ignoring the question.

"I've got a good mind to, little brother. However, momma beat you senseless already. It's not going to make any difference if I hit you," she laughed and shook her head.

When Ty turned back to the microwave, she twisted the towel and snapped it across his back end.

He turned around with quick enough reflexes to catch her before she ran from the room. Kissing her on the head, and giving her a tight hug, he expressed his affection for her.

"It's a good thing I love you, sis. How was my little girl today anyway?"

"Well, she didn't want to take a nap after school, so she'll probably fall asleep soon."

"Not before I get to spend some time with her first," he said taking the bowl from the microwave.

With one bite, he put the spoon back in the bowl and placed it on the shelf. His sister laughed to herself, and told him there was a plate for him in the oven, as she went to bathe her niece. She left the room shaking her head, but said nothing else.

Just as Ty finished his supper, Chantal came in, rubbing her eyes.

"It looks like my baby girl is tired. Are you ready for me to read you a story?"

"Okay, Papa," she said yawning and holding her arms out to him.

Their quiet time was short-lived, as Chantal fell sound asleep after only a few pages of her favorite story. Ty brushed her braids away from her face, kissed her, and tucked her in for the night. Shutting off the light on her nightstand, he picked up the picture of her mother and stared at it.

"Why?"

He placed the picture back in its place and went out, shutting the door slightly as he left.

"Well, I'm all done here, Ty. Unless there's anything else you need."

"No thanks, Denise. You've done more than enough. Besides, don't you have a date with your husband tonight," he smiled.

"Yes, as a matter of fact, I do and if I don't get upstairs soon, he'll come looking for me."

Chantal loved Saturday mornings because she was able to wake Ty. They would "wrestle" for a while, then get up and make breakfast together. Blueberry pancakes were her favorite, especially the whipped cream happy face Ty would put on top.

This Saturday was extra special though. Denise was taking her to buy a new dress for Sunday. She couldn't wait to go shopping with her. In her haste, she spilled some of her milk, trying to drink it too quickly.

"Whoa, take it, easy princess. You're going to choke if you don't drink slower. Don't worry; your aunt won't leave without you. Here, use your napkin. So, what color is this dress going to be," he asked as if she hadn't told him a thousand times already.

"Papa, you know I want to get a blue dress, just like the one on my doll. Do you think the store will have one like that?"

"Well, I don't know, but I'm sure you'll look beautiful in whatever color you get.

Now, why don't you put your things in the sink, and go brush your teeth, and wash your face and hands, do you need my help?"

"Nope, I'm a big girl now. I can do it all by myself. Want to see," she asked, as she took off for the bathroom.

Ty followed her, and wondered when she became so independent. After all, she was only six years old. She just started school two months ago. Where had the time gone? If only her mother could see her little girl right now, at this very moment. However, Ty knew that wasn't going to happen not now, not ever.

Ty arrived at the community center early; only to find the gymnastics class hadn't finished yet. After they moved the equipment out of the way, a few guys, who also coached, started to shoot some hoops, while waiting for all the players for the "big game" to arrive.

"Come on bro. What are you waiting for," they asked Ty.

"Excuse me if some of us would like to stretch before taking you on," he retorted.

Amanda Clarke, who was the gymnastics teacher, sat on the bleachers and finished her paperwork. She found her attention drawn to the nearby conversation. Looking up she saw Ty stretching and landing a split, almost to the floor. Very impressive she thought, but she wouldn't tell him for fear his ego might be inflated.

During the game, she saw the sweat glistening on his smooth brown skin, as he ran back and forth on the court. It wasn't until he sat on the bleachers below, and leaned back on his elbows, did she see his well-defined muscles. He had perfectly sculpted arms and shoulders. His physique showed that he was not a stranger to working out. His pectoral muscles along with his firm abdomen were visible through the sides of his jersey. As he lifted the jug of water to his lips, she noticed two more features, the thin mustache, and slight bit of hair below his bottom lip, and a bare ring finger on his left hand.

Being new to the community center, Amanda didn't know everyone who worked there yet. She didn't even know Ty's name. What did it matter anyway? They hired her to teach gymnastics, and that was all. Girding herself with resolve, she brought herself back to her senses. She couldn't afford the distraction of romantic notions. Between assisting the kindergarten teacher at the local elementary school, and working at the center, she didn't have time anyway. She finished recording the grades for her class, before leaving the center, and her thoughts of Ty far behind her.

Circumstances were such that the phone stopped ringing after Amanda finally unlocked the door and dropped her grocery bags on the kitchen table. Frustrated, she looked at the caller ID. It had been her father. She quickly called him back.

"Hey, dad, sorry I missed your call. I was just getting in the door. How are you," she asked.

"I'm doing great. And how is my girl?"

"I'm doing good, just trying to get used to being a Bostonian. This city takes some getting used to."

"I bet it won't take as long as you think. So any new love in your life yet?"

Hiding her exasperation she answered, "No daddy, I haven't found anyone like you yet."

"Give up trying honey. I'm one of a kind. When God made me, he broke the mold," he laughed. "Are you coming home for winter vacation?"

"I'm not sure, but I'll let you know. I'm just getting to know everyone, and beginning to fit in at work."

"Don't worry about it. I was just wondering. If not then, maybe we can do it sometime during the summer."

"As soon as I know, I'll call you. Oh, how is grandma doing?"

"She's holding her own as usual."

"Can you tell her I love her, and give her a kiss and hug for me?"

"I absolutely will do that for you. Well, I don't want to keep you. You sound tired."

"A little I guess. I'll call you soon dad. Love you."

Amanda felt bad about cutting the conversation short, but her dad was right.

She was tired. She removed the flowers from the cellophane wrapper, and prepared them for the vase. She was hopeful that their color would add some brightness to the otherwise dark kitchen. After setting them on the table, she smiled.

"There, that's a little better. Now, I had better eat something before I tackle those grant applications. Let's see, Chinese food sounds good. While I'm waiting for them to deliver it, I'll take a shower."

As the warm water caressed her tired body, Amanda thought about how she was going to make it in Boston. True, her life in California had been fast-paced, but now, she found it hard to make new friends, and came home every night to an empty apartment. Sometimes the silence was suffocating. She vowed to make at least one new friend during the following week.

The task proved to be a little easier than she thought. On Wednesday, Laurie, one of the other instructors at the center invited her to go to the bowling alley with them on Saturday night. She accepted, and found that the rest of the week went by quicker than usual. At least she wouldn't have to spend the entire weekend alone.

Everyone met at the bowling alley at seven. The 70's sound of ABBA singing Dancing Queen blared over the speakers. They purchased refreshments and snacks at the outset. Everyone split into two teams, and the fun began. Ty and Amanda walked up to the line for their turns simultaneously.

"Ladies first," he said and backed up.

With a deliberate casual movement, Amanda turned, and thanked him. She looked long enough to notice his attire, which consisted of a tan basketball jersey, tan pants, a black skullcap, and an eagle medallion. He looked fine. The tantalizing scent of his cologne found its way to Amanda, awakened her senses, and made her lose her train of thought. This resulted in only getting one pin down and nine to go.

"Oh well, I guess I'm out of practice."

Before taking her second turn, she let Ty take his first. STRIKE! It was going to be a long night, Amanda thought. Everyone was giving high fives, and a handshake that was new to her. She high-fived Ty but didn't quite get the handshake. He laughed and showed her again, before she took her turn. When she got the rest of the pins down, Ty was the first to congratulate her, and give her "dibs" as he called it. With a little practice, she'd get it right.

The rest of the night went by too fast. Even though she started behind him, she beat Ty's score by eleven on the first game. He, however, left her in the dust by forty, on the second one. It was still early enough when they finished, so the local pizza parlor received their patronage after the game.

Amanda talked with Laurie while Karen and Nancy kept to themselves. She managed to do this, while discreetly watching and listening to Ty. From a distance, the magnetism of his smile drew her. His teeth even and white, contrasted pleasingly with his dark skin. Tracing his other features with her eyes, she wondered if his high cheekbones suggested that he was part Native American.

Ironically and unknown to her was the fact that he was part Cherokee. His profile was sharp and confident.

She listened as he talked about his other job at the juvenile detention center and of course his favorite sport, basketball. His brown eyes grew wide with excitement. She tried not to be caught staring at him, but his return glances came back repeatedly. She offered him a small, shy smile. He responded with an upraised eyebrow before rewarding her with a larger smile of his own. This action of course sent her pulse racing. Biting her lip, she looked away.

He went back to the conversation leaving her to wonder if he was only mocking her. Either way, she decided that she would not permit herself to fall under his spell. After all, she came to Boston to find who she was, without any man interfering in that process. There was still a chance for her to grow completely again, and she didn't want to confuse things by getting involved with someone.

By midnight, they all started making their way home. Amanda knew it was going to be difficult making it to her Bible class in the morning. Nevertheless, she promised herself that she wouldn't use any lame excuses not to go. Being there tired, would be better than not being there at all. She could hear her grandmother's voice in her head, chiding her for coming in late.

It was difficult to get up the next day, but somehow she managed, despite the previous night's activities. She donned her aqua sleeveless empire-waist dress and matching jacket. It came to her ankles and fit her curves nicely. She arranged her long hair in a braid, with a matching ribbon bow fastened at the end. Her comfortable white pumps would be welcome during the ten-minute walk.

On the other side of town, Ty finished readying Chantal to go to services with Denise and her husband Roger.

"You look beautiful in your new dress sweetheart."

"Thank you, papa."

Denise walked in and inquired as to whether he would be joining them, the same as she did every Sunday. The answer was always the same. "Not this week." Denise had learned not to argue with Ty anymore.

For two years now, he refused to go. After his wife's death, he blamed God for taking her from him, and saw no point in it. Any time they spoke about Vanessa, there was a faint tremor in his voice, as the emotions touched him, and tore away at his heart.

There were nights when he cried out in pain for her; nights that he thought would never give way to morning. His grief at times prompted Denise to urge him to seek professional help, but each time he dismissed it.

Not wanting to taint Chantal's thoughts with his poisonous ones, he allowed her aunt and uncle to take her with them to services. When she wanted to talk about her mother, he tried to be positive, although there was a terrible sense of bitterness.

He had thought, by immersing himself with his full-time, third shift job at the youth detention center, and coaching would help to keep his mind occupied, and most of the time it did. There were times when he was alone, that the thoughts and images of Vanessa flooded his very being.

She was only twenty-three when her life ended, cut short by a co-worker who had fallen asleep at the wheel, killing both of them instantly. With Chantal being only four at the time, Ty had to raise her alone. Shortly after, Denise and Robert moved to the upstairs apartment, to help bring up their niece and treat her like their own daughter.

As the months past, winter turned into spring, then summer with vacation, and before they knew it, September, and a new school year. Autumn quickly became Amanda's favorite season, as she watched the leaves change from green into vibrant colors, something she hadn't experienced in California.

However, the leaves weren't the only things that had changed that autumn. Amanda and Ty drew closer to each other, the more time they spent together. It had still been in the company of their workmates, yet the process had begun.

On his way out of the center one afternoon, she nervously called him. He turned around, stopped midway from putting his jacket over his head, and left it on his forearms.

"What's up?"

Amanda came to his side. His muscles were in plain view and too close for comfort. A soft gasp escaped her as she forced herself to zero in on his face instead.

"I was just wondering … um … well actually …"

Why is it so hard to remain coherent when I'm next to him, she thought.

"Yes?"

"Could do me the favor of dropping these forms at the post office for me? I'm really in a hurry tonight. I have to get back to school for the children's dress rehearsal."

"No problem. Consider it done."

"Great thanks. Well, I have to go so I'll see you tomorrow. Thanks again."

In an instant, she was out the door, and Ty was left standing there shaking his head, and wearing a silly grin. She's a strange one, he thought, as he finished putting on his jacket.

"When, if ever, does a heart heal itself after a great loss," Ty wondered.

Everyone had been encouraging him to start dating again, but he didn't feel that he would ever be ready for that step. He still grieved over Vanessa too much, and he knew that no one would be able to take her place. The loneliness he felt was not strong enough to overpower the grief. He often thought of what it must be like for Chantal though, growing up without a mother. She had Denise he reasoned, she would do all right.

Another emotion added to his plight, when he saw Amanda. It had started as a twinge, but it steadily grew into attraction. The fight within him was great. Was he being disloyal to Vanessa by feeling this way? He knew deep down she would have wanted him to get on with his life. She would have been upset that he had gone three years already without even dating anyone. He tried to convince himself, but each time he failed, until one cold day in October.

It had been Indian summer for the past two weeks, but winter was waiting on the doorstep. Amanda and Ty left the center at the same time one evening. Unarmed for the nip in the air, Amanda shivered as they walked into the direction of the wind.

"Here, you look cold," Ty said to her, as he offered his jacket.

"I'll be all right. The train isn't far."

"Don't be silly. You're already getting goose bumps."

Ty slowly wrapped the jacket around her and found his arm lingering across her shoulder while she tried nervously to button it closed.

"Thank you," was all she managed to say.

"Amanda, that sounds so formal. Do you have any nicknames?"

"Well, my father sometimes calls me Mandy."

"Mandy. That's nice. What does your mother call you? Hopefully not late for dinner," he laughed.

"My mom died when I was nine, but she called me her Mandy Lee."

"Oh, I'm sorry. That comment was insensitive of me."

"You had no way of knowing. There's no apology needed."

"Can I ask you something?"

"Sure."

"What was it like growing up without your mom?"

"Well … dad did the best he could under the circumstances. He worked two jobs so I didn't see him as much as I would have liked. My grandmother was the one who brought me up for the most part. She'll be ninety this year. I can't wait to go home this winter vacation to see her. Besides, it's warmer in California than it is here in the winter. I found that out the hard way last year."

"Oh, you're a California girl huh? I guess this New England weather is quite a change for you then."

"I'm slowly getting used to it. Well, here's my train. Here, I don't want to forget to give you back your jacket," she said while she started to remove it.

"Hang on to it for now. You can give it back to me tomorrow."

"But …"

"Don't worry about it. I have my sweater and besides my blood has already adapted to this cold. Hurry, you're going to miss your train," he smiled.

"I'll see you tomorrow then," she responded as she boarded the train.

They waved simultaneously, as he watched her leave. Left standing on the platform, he immersed in his thoughts. For the rest of the evening, his thoughts were on Mandy, and the things she had revealed to him about herself. He was intrigued, and wanted to know more.

The next day Amanda forgot his jacket in the morning, but brought it to the bowling alley that night.

The game was different this time. The handshakes and "dibs" between them became more like holding hands. When Ty, who rarely bowled a gutter ball, did, Mandy commented that it wasn't his fault, but rather the lane was warped and caused it.

He smiled and asked, "Really? Is that what did it?"

The glow of his smile warmed her heart. The attraction she tried to ignore, broke through, and overtook her thoughts.

During the following week, she tried her hand at basketball so they would have something else in common. Not doing too well at first, Ty offered to show her how to play. Despite her mistakes, she persevered, being determined to learn to play the game well. It was difficult enough to get the ball from Ty, but keeping it from him proved even more challenging. After several weeks, her game improved, and Ty challenged her to yet another one-on-one game, after everyone had left for the night. To his surprise, she did a good job of keeping it from him.

"Hmm, I taught her too well," he thought to himself. "I need a new strategy."

"Do you know how attractive you look right now, Mandy?"

Surprised by this cunning diversion, she looked up, and lost the ball to him.

"That's a sneaky way to mess up my game Ty. That wasn't fair!"

With a mischievous look in his eyes, he replied, "All's fair in love and war."

She chased him down to the other end of the court to redeem herself.

"How can you even say that anyway? Look at me. My hair is all over the place. I'm all sweaty and God knows, I must smell!"

Ty stopped dribbling and laughed. Stopping short, she almost crashed into him.

"I am looking at you. That's why I said it. It means a lot to me that you'd take the time to learn a game that I love to play."

He brushed her hair away from her face.

"And even though you need a shower, no offense, I do find you very attractive."

"Thanks, but I wouldn't talk if I were you. No offense. Although... you're very attractive yourself."

Ty carefully pushed his thoughts of Vanessa aside just long enough to ask Amanda out. She accepted and they planned for Friday night.

When Ty arrived at Amanda's apartment, her transformation overwhelmed him. Tonight she wore a long black leather skirt, red v-neck chenille sweater with a black nylon tank underneath, and black suede ankle boots. Her silky chestnut hair flowed down to her waist. She wore just enough makeup and a simple silver herringbone around her smooth white neck. She heard his quick intake of breath. He was momentarily speechless, in his surprise.

"Hi," she said, speaking first.

"Hi," he answered in a calm voice, his gaze still fixed on her.

"Are you okay Ty?"

Breaking free from his dream-like state, he apologized for his rudeness, and inquired if she was ready to go. She left him at the door while, she retrieved her coat, and then they were on their way.

"Are you sure you're feeling okay," she asked as they started to walk to the restaurant.

"I'm fine. I'm just admiring how beautiful you look tonight."

Amanda's face turned a bright crimson color, as she bit her bottom lip.

"Thank you."

"I never realized how long your hair was."

"French braids can be very deceiving."

"I guess so, and the fact that I'm used to seeing you in sweats and sneakers. Not that there's anything wrong with wearing gym clothes, but you look so different. And you can only imagine if I found you attractive then how much more attractive I find you now."

"Stop it, Ty, you're embarrassing me," she laughed.

"There's nothing to be embarrassed about. Do you want me to change the subject?"

"That's a very good idea," she smiled.

We never finished talking about your family the other day. What are they like? Would your grandmother and father approve of us dating?"

"Considering the circumstances he was in when he fell in love with my mother, I'm sure he wouldn't object at all. You see, my mother's parents disapproved of her dating, let alone marrying my father. However, they were determined. After that, my grandparents had nothing to do with her, not even to come and visit when I was born. They actually saw me once with my mom in a shopping mall when I was about eight or nine. They acknowledged me but that was all.

When my mother died, they came to the funeral but blamed my father for taking her away in the first place. They felt that if she hadn't gone off with him, she would still be alive.

I remember being so angry with them for saying that to my father, so much so, that I started screaming at them. My face was beet red, and I could feel the blood pounding in my head. Then my father did something I couldn't understand at the time. He made me apologize to them. I refused at first, but when I saw the hurt in his loving eyes, I broke down and did what he asked, but I certainly didn't like it or mean it at the time."

"That must have been the hardest thing you had to do at that age," Ty said sympathetically.

"It was, but I learned that day that my father and grandmother never lashed out at anyone. They always told me to be proud of who I was, and not to let other people make me feel inferior. Most importantly, we should never return evil for evil. Treat them with kindness instead."

"That's not always an easy thing to do. Especially when it's God you're mad at," Ty said with his voice trailing off at the end.

Amanda turned to him, hoping he was going to elaborate. Instead, she found him with a far off look in his eyes. Chancing the answer, she encouraged him to explain just what he meant.

Ty tried to suppress the tormented feelings that welled up within him.

"I was married once, Mandy. Vanessa was the love of my life. One night, she and one of the girls she worked with were coming home from a double shift at the hospital. The other girl, Lorraine was driving, and she fell asleep at the wheel. She crossed over into oncoming traffic and hit a truck head-on."

He stopped, and took a long deep breath before continuing.

Amanda placed her hand within his for support.

"I'm so sorry Ty."

The tears fell as he continued.

"They were killed instantly. I never had the chance to say goodbye. Up until the funeral, I had been numb. At the funeral, the only thing the minister said that stayed with me was that God took her to be with him. From that day on, I blamed God for taking her away from our daughter and me. Why would he take a wonderful woman away from her husband and her little girl? Why do you think he would do that?"

Amanda wiped away her tears, and tried to compose herself before answering.

"Well ... from what I've learned from Bible class, God loves us, and doesn't take anyone to be with him in heaven. It's time and circumstances that come upon us which sometimes result in sicknesses or even death."

Ty looked up at her with swollen eyes. He grasped both of her hands within his.

"Do you really believe that," he asked sincerely.

"Yes, I do. Think about it, Ty. How can we base our faith in a God who would be so cruel that he would take our loved ones away from us? It doesn't make sense. Where is the love in that? God is the very epitome of love. Taking someone away would contradict everything he stands for, as does punishing anyone in a burning hellfire."

"I never thought about it that way. You know, it's going on three years, and all that time I haven't prayed about anything. I guess it's a combination of feeling betrayed and hypocritical, if I asked him for anything. Do you think he would listen to me after all this time, and with the attitude I've had toward him?"

"Ty, he's always there to listen to us. We just need to show our faith in him, that he will answer us, but remembering that in some instances, the answer may be 'no'."

"I don't know if I can accept that part, Mandy."

"That's where the faith comes into play. He helps us through the bad times so we can continue with our lives. Besides, you have a little girl who needs you to show her the way. How old is she Ty?"

"Chantal is going to be seven. Every time I look at her, I see Vanessa. My sister and her husband have been a big help to me in caring for her. She's a great kid, Mandy. I don't know what I'd do without her."

"I'd like to meet her sometime."

"I'm sure she'd enjoy meeting you too. You both have something in common, growing up without a mother."

"And we both have loving fathers, who are always there when we need them."

"Thanks. That means a great deal to me. I don't want to ruin our evening Mandy, but now that we're here, I don't feel like eating. I'm sorry."

"Don't be sorry. You didn't ruin anything. We've learned more about one another just walking here. What time is it anyway?"

"It's seven-thirty, why?"

"Would tonight be too early to meet Chantal?"

"Do you want to meet her tonight?"

"Well, if it's all right with you, I would like to."

"It's fine. Just let me call my sister and see if she's still awake."

The night proved to be a success, as Amanda met and conversed with Denise and Roger. Although she sat quietly on Ty's lap, Chantal took in all she could about Amanda, until her eyes wouldn't stay open any longer, and she fell asleep in his arms.

Ty asked her if she wanted to help him put her to bed. Denise and Roger decided it was time to take their leave, expressed their pleasure to meet Mandy, and hoped she wouldn't be a stranger. She thanked them and said she hoped to see them again soon.

As they tucked Chantal in, Amanda saw the picture of Vanessa on the night table, and picked it up.

"She was very beautiful," Amanda said.

"Yes, she was."

"I can see her features in Chantal, especially her eyes. She's a beautiful little girl. Vanessa would be proud of the way you've raised her," she whispered, while placing the photo back in its place.

Ty walked over and stood behind Amanda, encircling her with his strong muscular arms.

"Thank you, Mandy. You don't know how much those words mean to me."

He sweetly kissed the top of her head, drowning in the scent of her perfume. Never did he think anyone would be able to fill the void Vanessa left behind when she died.

As for Amanda, she had never felt this way before. For a long moment, she felt herself melting into him, not wanting him to let go.

They walked hand in hand back into the living room. Before they had time to think another thought Ty's arms came around her again, but this time she was facing him. He took her face in his hands. A faint light twinkled in the depths of his brown eyes. She trembled under his touch and felt her knees weaken as his mouth descended. First, he kissed her forehead, then the tip of her nose, and finally, he kissed her soft lips. Their consciousness seemed to ebb as a warm glow flowed through them. Amidst the happiness they shared, Ty's faith would experience a testing, much sooner than he expected.

When spring and love were in full bloom, everyone from their group at the center planned a hiking trip in the New Hampshire Mountains. To keep it competitive, it was the guys against the girls. Although Ty and Mandy wanted to hike together, they conceded.

It was a warm day and the sun shone brightly, until around two o'clock. The clouds started to roll in, as the sky darkened. Fearing the worst, everyone moved along more quickly to reach the destination. Had the unpredicted snowstorm held off just another thirty minutes or so, everyone would have arrived safely.

However, the guys, being ahead of schedule, were the only ones who reached the meeting place before the snow started to fall heavily. They figured the girls weren't far behind, so they waited. However, after that crucial half-hour passed, they became concerned the girls were lost in the blinding force of the storm. They decided to split up. Jack stayed there, while Michael and Shawn went to the nearest ranger station. Ty traveled solo back down the mountain.

Alone with his thoughts, his mind burned with the memory of the way Amanda looked on the night of their first "date." He had come to love and cherish her. He wanted to spend the rest of his life with her. As the storm worsened, he feared that his desires would never materialize.

The rangers quickly dispatched a search and rescue party. Within twenty minutes, they found Karen and Nancy, but Amanda and Laurie were still missing. They had some distance between them, as Laurie had fallen, and gashed her leg. Once the snow started to build up, she couldn't continue upward, so they agreed to go back down, and find shelter. Unfortunately, in doing so, they veered from the path, and became lost. Numbed from tiredness, the frigid wind, and her injury, Laurie gave up the idea of them finding their way out. Amanda reassured her either they would find shelter or someone would find them. She was certain Ty would find them or send out someone who could. Happening upon a small dugout shelter, they huddled together and prayed.

After retracing the trail, the girls were supposed to be on, and coming up empty, everyone surmised they unknowingly deviated from the path. With the information they acquired about Laurie's injury, things looked grave. Besides searching for the girls, the rangers now had to locate Ty. Going a little further down the mountain, they found him and relayed the bad news.

Realizing the situation was no longer in his hands, he prayed to the only one who could help him in his solitude. He remembered what Amanda said about God always answering prayers but sometimes the answer was "no." He erased the thought from his mind, and continued his search for them with renewed strength, both physically and spiritually.

The minutes seemed like hours, as the storm heightened. As time elapsed, the chances of finding them alive, if they found them at all, became increasingly slimmer. The menacing sound of the storm diminished the voices of those searching for them. The wind-driven snow stung their faces, yet they trudged ahead. Although their rescuers were getting closer, it was at the point where Amanda and Laurie were so cold; they began to drift in and out of consciousness.

The icy cold wind shifted to blow in their direction. Their shelter wouldn't help them much longer. Amanda fought back the desire to fall asleep, but Laurie had already succumbed to it. Looking out into the storm, Amanda thought she saw the outline of a man coming towards them. Could it be Ty, she thought. It must be. I knew he would find us. However, as the image began to fade, she thought maybe he couldn't see them. With all the strength she could muster, she called out his name and then surrendered to an unconscious state. Although the image she saw wasn't Ty, he was nearby, and heard her call out his name.

Rounding the almost buried dugout crag, Ty saw her face. He yelled for the others to come and help. Wrapping them tightly in blankets, and putting them on basket sleds, they brought them to the ranger station at the base of the mountain. While awaiting a rescue vehicle, they treated them for hypothermia, but neither regained consciousness.

Ty sat by Mandy's side, and prayed. The tears fell silently on the blanket, which formed her cocoon. She looked so tiny and helpless. Her color hadn't returned either. His mind raced, as his fears knotted inside him. He would go crazy if he lost her too. One tragedy like this in a lifetime was already too much to handle. Time was not in her favor. She needed to come out of it before it was too late.

Just when he thought he couldn't bear it any longer, the answer to his prayer became "yes." Her skin began to lose its bluish tint and started to pink up. Not having the full realization of her new surroundings, she fought against her protective wrapping.

"Hey, settle down. It's all right Mandy. You're safe now," Ty reassured her.

"Where are we," she asked trying to focus her vision on him.

"We're at the ranger station. You and Laurie got lost and…"

Mandy didn't let him continue before she jumped in.

"Laurie! Is she okay? I think she was unconscious. I tried to keep her awake."

Ty looked over at Laurie and saw that she was coming around as well.

"She's going to be alright. You both were unconscious when we found you. It's a good thing you stumbled upon the makeshift shelter. Without it, I don't think you would have been as fortunate," Ty replied, as he turned his face from her view.

"We prayed too. That's what kept us protected," she whispered.

"I was praying the entire time too. I've never prayed so hard in my life. What you told me about the answers to prayers kept coming back to me. I don't know what I would have done had the answer been no. I don't know if I would have had the faith and stamina to go on with my life. Besides Chantal, you are the essence of my very being. I love you and I want you to be my wife and Chantal's mom if you'll have us."

The tears glistened on her pale, heart-shaped face, as the warmth slowly crept back into her body. Her exhausted eyes smiled at him.

"That would be the answer to my prayers, Ty. There's nothing more that I could ask for in this world than to be a part of your family."

After a full recovery, the wedding plans began with Denise's help, and the loving guidance of Amanda's grandmother. Amanda wore her mother's wedding dress. Everyone commented on her glowing appearance.

Ty made a handsome groom, as he stood awaiting her arrival by his side. Chantal was the perfect little flower girl, spreading rose petals, as she walked gracefully down the aisle. While giving her away, Amanda's father told her that he was glad she found a good man.

Amanda stood beside her husband to be, and they became lost in each other's eyes. At the appropriate moment, they kissed. It was a kiss as tender and light as a summer breeze. It sealed their vow, and left a promise of the primary image of love's gift to them as husband and wife.

## Tangible Dreams

As Christian Miguel Dominguez strode across the floor, it creaked under his muscular frame. His olive skin was smooth, even though much of his time he spent outdoors in the hot summer sun. The glass of red wine glistened from the flickering light of a single candle that was beside it on the mantelpiece. Lifting it with one hand, he artfully ran the other through his hair, and then over his face. Staring thoughtfully at his reflection, he decided he was pleased with this new look. The fine sideburns, mustache, and goatee suited him.

While finishing the last taste of the harvest, he extinguished the almost nonexistent candle, removed the CD from the stereo, and meticulously placed it in the leather case. As he continued to the bedroom, he felt the familiar emptiness, an emptiness that had only recently begun to gnaw within him. Sleep came quickly, for the events of the day and effects of the wine overpowered him.

She came softly into his dream. Tonight she wore a blue silk gown with a matching wrap that was drawn over her arms. She remained barefoot, as always. Her waist-length hair flowed like the waves of the sea. Sitting on the blanket spread before them, she motioned for him to join her. Tonight, as every night, he reclined with his head in her lap. While she ran her slender fingers through his tousled mane, he told her what he had accomplished that day. She listened closely, never uttering a word. Her gentle caress took away the pain, which engulfed his soul and filled it instead with light and happiness. Her smile melted his heart, and made him wish that morning would never come. Yet, each night would end, and she would depart, leaving him longing for the daylight hours to disappear, so that he could be with her again.

Christian led an uncomplicated life. He rose at six a.m. every morning. Since he wasn't a stranger to hard manual labor, his mason and carpentry skills served him well. Long hours left him satisfied with his work, but exhausted by evening. A nightly pattern of dinner, a massaging shower to soothe his aching muscles, a glass of wine coupled with a good book, and a selection of music, left him ready to retire at ten p.m.

He earned good pay as a skilled artisan, which afforded him a house on the beach. However, he wanted more in his life, even if it meant leaving Los Alamitos to find it.

Needing a change, he left Venezuela for the States just ten years before. He regularly sent money home to his family, along with gifts throughout the year, but had only been home once to visit.

There were as many reasons to stay, as there were to leave his country, but he felt leaving would serve him better. It had, up to this point in his life. Even though he had the things he wanted materially, it still left him wanting someone with whom to share it. The one woman that haunted his dreams every night, would be the only woman he could ever completely love though, and yet she remained absent from his life.

Elizabeth Anne Fitzgerald put in a long 48 hours, trying to finish her project for the International Traveler magazine.

She went over the photos many times, so in order to match the best ones with the written text. She made the final decision, placed everything in her portfolio, and began to prepare for what she thought was a decent night's sleep. She shuffled around the apartment, checking that she locked the door, and shut off all the lights. The bathroom floor was cold on her feet. She washed off what was left of her makeup, and brushed her teeth. Her hair was up for hours, and it made her headache to take it down.

She awoke with a start, after only two hours of restless slumber. The clock read 1:25 a.m.

Rising from the bed, she pulled back the sheer curtains; revealing a full moon hanging lazily in the sky. Unable to sleep, she took her journal from the nightstand and wrote down the only details of the dream that she could remember.

Cold, windy, dark ominous skies, walking in my nightshirt, searching, trying to call out, but the wind had taken my voice, and whipped my hair against my face.

Night after night, she had a similar dream. Every morning left her with the same questions. What did it all mean? Where was she, and for whom was she searching?

Elizabeth walked toward the head office to receive an assignment from her obnoxious boss, Mr. Richard Sinclair III. She could see him through the window, flailing his hands in the air, as he spoke to one of her colleagues.

As she entered the room, he paused for a split second, and then resumed the conversation just as quickly, while sliding the manila folder across the table. It stopped just short of flying off and onto the floor. Just to be sure, she saved it from a fatal end; Elizabeth slammed her hand down on top of it.

"You're so subtle Richard."

"I just wanted you to get started A.S.A.P. We're two days behind schedule as it is now. I hope you have your bags packed, because the plane leaves at 1500 hours."

"Four and a half hours? Well, I'm glad warm climates don't require much clothing."

"Oh, on the contrary Lizzy, you'll need extra clothes where you're going."

"Don't call me Lizzy! And just where are you sending me, Siberia?"

"Close, very close. Alaska to be exact, and you better be back in this office within the allotted time or you will be in Siberia."

"You're so good to me. How can I ever thank you," she remarked sarcastically as she stormed out the door.

"Have a nice trip...Lizzy."


"Elizabeth, wait," Stephanie called from her little cubicle in the corner.

"I'm kind of in a hurry Stephanie. No thanks to our fearless leader."

"That's what I wanted to talk to you about. You got the Alaska assignment right?"

"Do you have to rub salt in the wound, Steph?"

"Actually...I have a proposition for you."

"What, we send Sinclair instead," she laughed.

"No, send me instead, and you can take my assignment."

"You want to go to Alaska? Where are you sending me then?"

"How does Venezuela sound?"

"Are you serious? Oh, Stephanie, you're the best. Now we just have to let the boss know," she winced.

"No problem girl. He owes me from a previous assignment. I'll be right back. Wait here. Better yet, can you go downstairs and get me a latte at the coffee shop?"

They confirmed the arrangements, and Elizabeth had more time to pack, as she was leaving at 8 p.m. now.


On the plane, she looked through the portfolio. For this assignment, she was determined to prove herself as a professional photographer. She would capture the essence of every place assigned for her to visit. For now, though, she could relax.

Positioning the seat just right, she fell into a twilight sleep, but deep enough for her to dream her all too familiar dream. The light hurt her eyes, as she strained to see the figure before her. It was the outline of a muscular frame. As her eyes adjusted, the outline became a shadow with a little more definition, so that she could distinguish his features slightly. However, he disappeared as quickly as he had appeared, leaving her to wake with a shudder.

Christian had just emerged from the shower, when the telephone rang. He wrapped himself in a towel, and ran across the cold tile floors of the bathroom and kitchen. He picked up just as the caller was about to disconnect.

"Hello? Papa, what's wrong? Did something happen to mama?"

"No Christian, it's Jorge again. Can you please come home?"

"Yes, I will be home as soon as I can.

"Thank you, my son, thank you."

"Again," he said as he placed the receiver back on the cradle.

"How much longer will this go on before the inevitable happens? Mama cannot have much strength left to deal with this, and papa is running out of options. I must do whatever it takes to care for this situation."

He called the airport and scheduled a 7 a.m. flight, reserved his rental car, packed his valise, and went to bed. He would be home soon he thought, as he went to sleep. As always, he dreamt of her. Tonight though, she would be standing alone, without him, staring into the skies as his plane left her behind.

The airport was bustling with passengers coming and going. Christian made his way to the rental car desk, and picked up the keys to his jeep. It was a two and a half drive to the tiny village where he grew up with his brother and twin sisters. It had been six years since he had been home. He was looking forward to seeing his parents and "little" sisters.

The thought of an encounter with Jorge was not a pleasant one. How would he find him this time? His situation had worsened, judging by the sound of his father's voice last night. How would he handle it? He tried to shake it, but he knew that he had to come to grips with it before he went to see him.

As he rounded the last curve before his parents' house, he took a deep breath. Pulling into the yard, he saw his sisters taking in the wash from the line. Luisa was the first to see him as he was getting out of the jeep.

"Juanita, look; it's Christian!"

Juanita dropped the towel that she was folding and both girls ran to him. He put down his luggage and caught both of them in his arms. The three of them fell up against the jeep, yet continued embracing. Kissing them on their foreheads, he exclaimed, "I cannot believe how much you two have grown from little girls to young ladies."

The two of them giggled, and kissed their brother with the affection that only sisters can give their oldest brother and mentor.

"We've missed you, Poochy," cried Juanita, using their nickname for him.

"Yes, so much," agreed Luisa.

"Poochy? Well, it's certainly been a long time since anyone has called me that. I'd almost forgotten."

Before he could say another word, his mother saw him through the kitchen window and called to him.

Christian ran inside to meet her.

"Mama," he cried as he gingerly picked her up and hugged her.

"I have missed you so much, mama!"

With tears in her eyes, she returned the embrace.

"You are home my son. How long will you stay? Are you hungry? Come into the kitchen. I just made paella. Here sit. Eat, eat!"

She promptly escorted him to the table, pulled out a chair, and sat him down.

He laughed his hearty laugh, "All right mama, all right. How have you been? Papa said..."

"Not today, mio. Tomorrow please, for today we will be happy. I am well though.

"Yes, then if we are to be happy, I must give you a present that I have brought for you."

As he went to his luggage, she exclaimed, "Mio, you spoil me; sending gifts all the time. It is not right...But I do love them," she laughed.

Of course, his sisters had perfect timing and walked in the door, when their gifts had only seconds before placed on the table. The laundry took secondary place to this event, and the baskets found a resting spot in the middle of the floor.

"Girls...the clothes!"

Obediently, they stopped in their tracks, and retreated to put the baskets in a strategic place before they ran back into the kitchen to receive their little treasures.

At precisely the same moment, their father entered the kitchen from the opposite doorway.

"Well...I see you are home my son. That is good. There is much you need to do, for example..."

"Pablo! Not now, tomorrow," his wife pleaded.

"Tomorrow, tomorrow, what if tomorrow doesn't come?"

"Then we have no need to worry about it."

Christian and the girls silently laughed in the corner, out of their father's sight; or so they thought.

Mrs. Dominguez walked over to her son and kissed him on the head.

"Everything will be all right, now that you are home."

Then playfully swatting the girls with her dish towel, she smiled, and sent them to put the laundry away in their respective rooms. They thanked Christian for their gifts and returned to their chores.

Elizabeth arrived in Venezuela several hours before Christian, and went to find her hotel, or posada. It wasn't the most luxurious, but then again she was working for a new company, which was trying to make its place in the travel world. One could say it was comparable to the cozy bed and breakfast inns of the States, but without the breakfast.

She slept for most of the trip, so a shower and a clean outfit prepared her for the first day of "work." She couldn't wait to get started. She carefully placed everything in her knapsack, the brochures, camera equipment, tokens, transportation information, identification, and journal. She hung her camera around her neck.

She wrote a list of stops, in logical order, and put the notebook conveniently in her denim shirt pocket. Taking an apple from the fruit basket in her room, she was on her way.

There were so many places to visit and she was looking forward to almost all of them. The idea of taking the longest and highest tramway in the world wasn't first on the list. It would certainly add much to the portfolio, yet she wasn't crazy about being at an altitude of 4,765 m, for a length of 12 km, in a little cable car!

There were many parks to visit and enjoy Poet's Park, Mother's Park, and Humboldt Park. Of course, the park dedicated to the famous Don Quixote and the Plaza Bolivar, where one could enjoy free concerts, was definitely on her list.

Elizabeth thoroughly enjoyed the Cultural Center, which housed the State Symphony Orchestra. The artisans, craftsmen, and women she observed not only worked with their hands, but also their hearts, in creating beautiful, timeless masterpieces.

At an art gallery, one artist in particular piqued her interest. It was an exhibit by Manuel Arjona. It featured paper and glue art, which he interestingly called 'Sueños del Papel' (Paper Dreams).

The quote under his name read the following: "This material is human-like, smooth when new, and wrinkled when old. If you leave it, it will disappear. If you care for it, and nurture it, it will survive."

"How simplistic, yet clever," she thought, 'Paper Dreams.'

The day was not as exciting for Christian, as his papa succeeded in speaking with him before it was over, although not within earshot of his mama. He told him of his brother's grave situation. For the past eighteen months, he had been playing the role of the prodigal son, at the point where he had not yet returned. He had stolen money from his parents, and squandered it on a life of drinking, gambling, and getting into quite a bit of trouble with the authorities. Not to mention the fact, his laziness and dishonesty cost him his well-paying job.

His parents were at their wit's end in knowing what to do with him, besides the fact that it left them in jeopardy of losing their home. If that happened, his mother would be heartbroken; for it was the home, where she grew up. She inherited it when her parents died, just six months before she wed.

"I don't know what else to do Christian. We are not even sure where he is at this moment."

"Don't worry papa. I will find him and fix this situation. This house will not be lost! The girls do not know that it has come to this, do they?"

"Your mama and I have tried to hide as much of this as we can from them. They are very smart girls. I think they may be hiding how much they understand from us."

"Yes, they are very intelligent. They are growing up so fast. Before you know it they will be starting families of their own."

"Hopefully, but if this terrible shame continues on this house... well.... I'm not sure that they will be able to become wives of respectable men."

"By the time they are ready papa, this situation will be long gone and forgotten. I promise you that. Now, before we retire for the night, let us concentrate on something less stressful, a game of chess perhaps?"

"How is playing a chess game with you not stressful?"

They both began to laugh as Isabel came into the room. After putting some refreshments before them, she commented on their jovial attitudes.

"I am glad to see that you are not discussing anything that can wait until the morning. Before you start your game, the girls would like to come in and say goodnight."

After competing for three hours, all their spent strategy ended in a stalemate. They retired for the night, but sleep eluded Christian for a few more hours. He spent the night planning his tactics for the next day, at the very least, if he couldn't find Jorge that easily.

When he did fall asleep, it was fitful, and without dreams. The hours went by too quickly, and the morning light, although existent, was dull. It brought the thick fog and by six o'clock, a soaking rain.

"Great," Christian thought. "Why not make this day even more miserable than it has to be."

As he got dressed, he could smell the freshly brewed coffee wafting upwards. The scent of fresh-baked bread accompanied it, and beckoned him downstairs.

"Did you sleep well, mio," his mother inquired as she placed his breakfast before him.

"Hmm, it took me a while to get used to my old bed again. It was fine though."

"Your father told me that he spoke with you last night."

"Yes mama, he did. I am going to start by going to some of Jorge's old friends, to see if they know anything."

"Please be careful, mio. I don't want to lose you too."

"Don't worry mama. I will come back safely. That is my promise to you."

Christian finished his meal and started on the mission to find his younger brother. Some of the places he found himself were not the kinds of "establishments" that he ever frequented; except when searching out his brother's whereabouts. The characters that he met would never set foot in his house, at least not invited anyway. He wondered why Jorge chose his involvement in these sorts of affairs.

At one of his brother's old hangouts, he came across someone who everyone called "El Toro Silencioso" (The Silent Bull). This name described the way he would silently stalk, and then come up behind his prey, without them even suspecting his presence. His attack was like a raging bull, stopped by no one.

Fortunately for Christian, he knew him before this reputation was cast upon him. He had helped rescue him from an industrial accident years ago. For this, Pedro, a.k.a. El Toro Silencioso, was forever in his debt. He told Christian that if he ever needed anything, he could rely on him to see it through. At the time, Christian never thought he would have needed him to help find and bring his brother to justice.

Pedro saw Christian out of the corner of his eye, and made his way across the crowded room. First, a slap on the back, then a bear hug, greeted Christian. Then they walked over to a table in the corner of the room, to talk. They decided that El Toro take over the search; since going any further, would put Christian in too much danger. He agreed to contact him when he found Jorge, and Christian would meet them somewhere safe. The two men shook hands on the deal, and Christian left to go home and wait for the call.

On the way, he stopped to buy flowers for his mother and sisters. A sigh of relief came over his mother's face as he walked into the house. Since the girls were present, they mentioned nothing about the day's events. Later in the evening, he divulged only some of the information, so as not to worry them or put them in jeopardy, if they asked questions.

The next day he had the needed money wired, to him to pay off his brother's debts and keep his parents from losing the house. He would deal with financial matters, when he and Jorge met face to face.

That meeting came sooner than he thought. At 1 p.m. that afternoon, the phone rang. Jorge was in jail, incarcerated for an earlier crime, just twenty miles outside the city. The drive was short, the confrontation shorter.

Christian hardly recognized Jorge. His younger brother of five years looked ten years older than he did. His face had scares and bruises in several places. He had lost so much weight, it seemed. Before he could even say anything, Jorge stopped him in his tracks.

"Well, if it isn't my American brother. It's been a long time, but not long enough. I don't suppose you came all this way to bail me out of here. That's just fine with me. I don't need your help anyway. Never did. Whatever I did to prove myself wasn't good enough for papa or mama either. I decided I didn't need them. I...."

Christian cut him off.

"It's amazing how you needed their money though, and used it without thinking of anyone but yourself. Did you stop to think or care that they are soon going to be without the house where we grew up? Do you care that mama's health has worsened because of your actions, or that papa is at his wits end with all the bills, and not enough money to pay them? And the girls...."

"As usual everything is my fault. I'm sick to death of being everyone's scapegoat. And don't even talk to me about your sisters."

"My sisters? Since when are they just my sisters? Have you disowned them too? I swear if I ever find out that you have put them or mama and papa in any physical danger I'll..."

"You'll do what? Please, save your breath for someone who wants to hear it. As far as I'm concerned, this conversation is over. You can put yourself in the same boat as they are for all I care. You are not my brother and I don't need you to come all this way from your precious house in the States to tell me how to run my life. I will never bother your family again, not even to get back what is rightfully mine. At least I got something out of the deal. I won't be here for long. But you can be sure that when I get out, I will never step foot in that house or contact them ever again!"

Before Christian could say another word, Jorge disappeared through the security doors. He decided to speak with the warden to see how long Jorge would be there, before going home and breaking the news to his parents.

He was so enraged with his brother's attitude. Letting it get the better of him, he paid little attention to his driving. It was getting dark and the roads were winding. As he came around a blind curve, his senses returned. He had crossed over to the other side of the road, in the path of an oncoming vehicle. He swerved back just in time. Another second and it would have proven deadly for both drivers. The vehicles came to screeching halts on opposite shoulders.

Christian jumped out of his jeep and ran across to the other driver. She wasn't hysterical as he thought. Instead, he found her in a state of shock. She was staring straight ahead, her knuckles white from her tight grip on the steering wheel.

"Miss, are you all right?"

When the young woman turned to face him, he saw the tears streaming down her face, although she didn't utter a sound.

"I am so sorry. It was entirely my fault. But I need to know if you are all right."

Somehow, his words reached more than her ears this time, and she shook herself out of her catatonic state.

"I'm all right. I think," she said calmly.

When she looked up at him, he saw a laceration on her forehead and blood was running down the right side of her face. He took his handkerchief out of his pocket.

"You're bleeding. Here let me get that for you."

After clearing away the blood, the gash proved to be minor.

"There, that's a little better. My sincerest apologies, I should have been paying more attention to my driving. A situation that I just left had me preoccupied."

"Another accident," she asked.

"What? Oh, no, a meeting with someone which didn't prove to be as productive as I would have liked. Anyway, are you sure you are all right?"

"Yes, just a little dazed. I was going back to the hotel anyway. I'll just rest there. Can you tell me the best way to get to El Patio?"

"Well I can tell you, but would you permit me to show you? That way I will feel better knowing that you arrived safely."

"I guess that would be okay," she said with a half-smile.

"Glad I can be of some service since I did cause the problem."

Elizabeth followed Christian to the hotel. He jumped out, opened her door, and held his arm out to help her. Feeling embarrassed, she declined his arm and said she could make it on her own from there.

"Well again, I am very sorry. By the way, my name is Christian Dominguez. Here is my phone number. If you need anything or need to go for medical care, please let me know. I will take care of any charges you may incur."

"That's very kind of you, Mr. Dominguez. But I don't think it will be necessary."

"Please, call me Christian. I feel like an old man when someone calls me Mr. Dominguez."

"Very well, Christian, I'm Elizabeth Fitzgerald. I wish that we met under better circumstances, but it was nice to meet you, and thank you for making sure I got here safely."

"Yes, I wish the situation had been different too. However, meeting you was my pleasure. Remember, I'm at your service."

"Thank you. Good-bye."

"Good-bye."

Christian waited until Elizabeth went to the front desk and then disappeared out of sight.

Early the next morning, as Elizabeth was getting ready to go out, there was a knock at the door. When she opened it, the hotel clerk was standing there with a beautifully decorated crystal vase overflowing with two dozen white roses.

"Miss Fitzgerald?"

"Yes?"

"These were delivered for you this morning."

"Who delivered them?"

"The florist delivered them, of course. Where would you like me to put them?"

After he had left, she looked to see if there was a card. She found it among the arrangement of flowers, ferns, and baby's breath. Sitting on the edge of the bed, she opened the envelope and read its contents.

'I just wanted to apologize again Miss Fitzgerald. I hope this morning's light found you feeling better and well rested. Your humble servant, Christian Dominguez'

Elizabeth laughed at the humble servant part but found it sweet that he would go to this length for someone he had never met before, especially when everything was fine.

She decided to call him and thank him.

"Hello," answered a young woman's voice on the other end.

It took Elizabeth off guard. As a result, she didn't respond fast enough before the voice spoke again.

"Hello? Is anyone there?"

"Oh, yes. I'm sorry. Is this the Dominguez residence?"

"Yes."

"I'm looking for Mr. Christian Dominguez please."

"Who's calling please?"

"This is Miss Fitzgerald."

"One moment please."

While she was waiting, for what seemed a very long time, Elizabeth wondered if she had walked into a bad situation. As she was contemplating hanging up, Christian picked up the receiver.

"Hello, Miss Fitzgerald. How are you?"

"I'm fine thank you. The roses are beautiful, but you shouldn't have gone to all that expense."

"Not at all, it was just my way of apologizing for everything that did, and could have happened yesterday."

"Well thank you, and... I hope I didn't cause any trouble for you by calling?"

"Trouble, why would you think that?"

"Well...it was a woman that answered, and I thought..."

"You thought it was... my sister, yes?"

"I...yes, your sister, of course. Well, again, thank you for the flowers."

"You're very welcome."

"Well I've taken enough of your time, and I do have to get going with my work."

"So you are here for work and not pleasure?"

"It's a little of both. You see, I'm a photographer for International Traveler. I get to experience and enjoy the sights of your wonderful country while I'm working. That's the beauty of this profession."

"Would it be too imposing of me to ask if you would like a tour guide to go with you? I know a good one that doesn't charge too much."

"Exactly how much does he charge?"

"Let me see. Today is Thursday. It must be your day because Thursdays are free!"

Both of them laughed at the same time.

"I couldn't possibly give up an offer like that one. How soon can you be here?"

"Is ten minutes too soon?"

"Let's make it fifteen."

"Great. I'll see you in the lobby in fifteen minutes then."

Since Elizabeth still had places to see in Merida, so this is where they started. Of course, she had to admit that she hadn't been on the cable car ride, Teleferico. Instead of going straight to the top in about an hour, they stopped at each of the four sections.

The scenery beneath them was picturesque. Rich flora with its vibrant reds, yellows, and purples shone brilliantly in the mid-morning sunshine. The landscape itself carefully hid the mountain lion, jaguar, and the tiny but melodious sounding tree frog from curious onlookers.

As they went along, Elizabeth listened to the stories and explanations of her tour guide while she captured the breathtaking images of El Gigante Dormido (the Sleeping Giant), Pico Espejo (Mirror Peak), Cerro El Leon (Lion Mountain), and the two lagoons named La Negra and La Colorado.

El Gigante Dormido is a mountain range that looks like a giant lying down on his back. Mirror Peak is its name because of the kind of stone you find at the top of it. The stone is Mica Moscovita. It is extremely bright, and when the sun shines on it, it produces the same reflection as a mirror.

They reached the third section of the tramway, Loma Redonda. This was the point where the cold and the height started to set in. They put on their jackets, got some hot chocolate, and slowed down the pace.

After a short rest, the journey continued to the summit, where everyone disembarked, and left the station to go to the viewing area. This is where they saw the statue of the Virgen de Las Nieves (the Virgin of the Snow).

In this area, they were able to see Pico Bolivar (Bolivar's Peak), which looked so close from that vantage point. Christian was quick to point out that although it "looked" close; it was a six-hour walk just to reach it. Not to mention it was outstanding emotional and physical conditions this kind of an excursion demanded. They decided to forgo this rigorous expedition, for the time being at least.

Taking the faster way down to where the trip began, allowed them to have lunch at one o'clock, instead of three or later. It was as hearty as it was filling. This gave them renewed strength with which to go exploring the Mercato de Principal (Principal Market). Here, one could find several wonderful treasures, which represented the beautiful country of Venezuela or "Little Venice," as its discoverer named it many years before. He remembered Venice when he arrived, as they built some of the thatched huts on stilts in the water.

Elizabeth had several friends and family to buy gifts for, and this seemed like the perfect place to start. One of her friends had requested a ruana, a colorful woolen poncho that adorns the people who live there.

For others, she chose several woodcarvings and finely decorated pieces of pottery. She splurged on herself and purchased a soft, warm, exquisitely made ecru sweater.

Christian also bought some artwork to bring back to the States. He felt closer to his home and family when he surrounded himself with artifacts from his native culture and heritage.

After they finishing shopping, Christian suggested that they bring the gifts back to the hotel for safekeeping.

"I had a wonderful day Christian," Elizabeth said, breaking the two-minute silence.

"I did too."

"Thank you for the tour. Work was never so much fun."

"Well, the fun doesn't have to stop here. If you want to go dancing tonight, I know a great place we could go to."

"Dancing? I haven't been dancing in a very long time."

"Then here's your chance," Christian smiled.

"I'd have to change, but I'll take you up on the offer. What time should I be ready for?"

"That all depends on whether or not I can take you to dinner first."

Elizabeth laughed. "You're very sly Mr. Dominguez, very sly."

"Does that mean yes then," Christian asked wide-eyed.

"Yes. What time should I be ready for?"

"I'll pick you up at seven. Do you need help with all these bags," Christian asked as they pulled into the parking lot of the hotel.

"No thank you. There's not that many. See you at seven then."

When they met again, Christian couldn't believe the transformation. Elizabeth wore a black handkerchief dress. Her hair hung down almost to her waist; where earlier it had been in a French braid. The gold hoop earrings she donned caught the light as she came down the stairs. Her wrap was around her but placed slightly below her shoulders. A small purse was in her right hand, as she needed her left to hold onto the railing on the staircase.

Christian's first reaction as she arrived at his side was a combination of shock and surprise.

"Wow! You look radiant!"

"And you look surprised," she responded.

"I am, no, I mean compared to earlier today you..."

Elizabeth playfully gave him an "excuse me look." At this point, she had Christian stumbling for words.

"Not that you weren't radiant earlier, it's just that you were dressed in jeans and ...well, now you're not. So what I mean to say is that you're more radiant now than before."

Christian ended with a sigh of relief, after finally articulating the thought he wanted to convey. He had hoped that it had not come across as insulting.

"Thank you. You look very handsome yourself, despite the red color on your face."

They both laughed and concluded that they had better leave the hotel if they were going to get to dinner on time.

The restaurant was warm and dimly lit. The concierge sat them at a table in the back near a little window, which had the view of the water. The light of the moon sparkled across the waves. There were so many items on the menu from which to choose.

The final choices were shrimp cocktail, salad with sliced cheese and tomatoes, clam soup, mackerel complemented by mixed vegetables, and a bottle of fine white wine. This left little room for dessert, so they decided against it.

After dinner, they still had time to sit and talk before going on to the dance hall. Here, they learned a little more about each other, since during day they mostly talked about the places they visited.

They arrived at the dance hall at around ten. Sounds of Latin music emanated through the open doors. They found room on the crowded dance floor, and became part of the festive crowd right away. The nighttime turned into morning, yet the music and dancing continued, from salsa and meringue to tango and bolero. Exhaustion set in around two, and the tired couples made their way to their respective vehicles.

"I want to thank you for the wonderful evening," Elizabeth said as she got out of the car at the hotel.

"The pleasure was all mine," Christian replied with a sincere look in his eyes.

"So you're leaving to go back to California tomorrow," Elizabeth asked with a sound of disappointment.

"Unfortunately, yes. I have some unfinished business to attend to here, and then I need to get back. I was hoping you could have met my parents and my sisters. You know, come to think of it, my mother's name is Isabel. In English, it's Elizabeth. What were the chances of that? Anyway, we have each other's phone number, address, and e-mail, so there'll be no reason why we can't get in contact. Maybe you can come to California or I can come to New York, depending on our schedules."

"I'd like that very much. I'll give you a call once I get back to the office and figure out my schedule. I think I might even have some vacation time I can use."

"Great. Let me know as soon as you can," Christian said, moving closer to her.

"Who would have thought an almost near-death experience would have brought us here," teased Elizabeth.

"So you're thanking me for that incident now?"

"I guess I am, in a way," Elizabeth smiled.

"Thank you for not getting hysterical and calling the police on me," Christian laughed.

"You are most welcome," Elizabeth replied.

"Well, good night, Elizabeth."

"Good night, Christian. Have a safe flight back."

"You as well," he answered and kissed her on the cheek, before smiling a devilish smile, and waving as she walked into the hotel.

While Christian returned home the next day, Elizabeth remained in Venezuela for another week. Nine days and thirty-five rolls of film later, she arrived back in New York.

There were several messages from Christian on her answering machine. She called to let him know that she was home, but was only able to leave him a message.

Unfortunately, her vacation time had to be set aside until she met an urgent deadline with the Venezuela article. In the meantime, the two played telephone tag with the answering machines.

It had been over a month since that night in Merida. Christian had hoped to speak with Elizabeth, even if they weren't able to see each other. However, this night, like many before, he only received a discouraging message.

"Christian, its Elizabeth. How are you? I'm fine, but I'm sorry to report that my boss has sent me on another assignment, this time to China. I'm due back in three weeks. Maybe we can get together then. I hope all is well with you and your family. Speak soon."

Disappointed, Christian ate little for dinner, took a shower, and went straight to bed. It wasn't long before he began dreaming about Elizabeth. The dream quickly switched gears though, and he saw the woman who had evaded his dreams for several weeks now. Something was different about her this night. She came to him and allowed him to tell her his thoughts as usual, yet she seemed distant. Christian felt that he had hurt or insulted her, but she would not speak to tell him so. This made the rest of the night fitful for him. He tossed and turned all night and woke up several times. By morning, he was more exhausted than the night before.

Elizabeth too was disappointed that they couldn't be together. However, what could she do when she had this assignment to fulfill? After all, it was her job, and she did enjoy it. It was too bad that it cut into her personal life. She hadn't noticed it so much when her life just included herself. Now she wanted to spend some time with Christian and that was impossible, at least for now. All she could hope for is that he would still be waiting when she returned.

Her dreams revived; she could now add a face to the outline. Yes, it was Christian's face. Still, he was so far away that she could not reach out and touch him. The wind took away her voice, as she called out his name. Then, as fast as he appeared, he was gone, leaving her to awaken with tears in her eyes, and a pain in her heart.

She finished out her three weeks and headed home. As soon as she arrived, she called him. Unfortunately, the recorded message she heard was not Christian's.

"The number you have called has been temporarily disconnected at the owner's request. No further information is available."

Elizabeth dialed it again to make sure that she hadn't made a mistake. Again, the same message came on. She listened to her messages to see if there was one from Christian. To her surprise, there wasn't. Had he given up on her that easily? Would she ever hear from him again? With a heavy heart, she went to the bedroom and unpacked her luggage.

Going through the gifts she bought, she came across the one she had bought for Christian. She wondered if it would ever find itself on a shelf in his house. Then she thought, "Why don't I mail it to him?" She wrapped it and addressed it to him; sending it out that afternoon. However, unbeknownst to her, it wouldn't reach its destination for some time.

Christian went to the post office to retrieve the mail, which they held for the past two and a half months. Among the many bills and letters, was a parcel from New York. Without looking at any of it, he put everything on the seat next to him.

The past few months had left him despondent and depressed. Not long after he arrived back in the States he had to sell his house. The money needed to save his parents' house and pay the bills his brother accrued in their name depleted the funds that he had put aside. He moved into an apartment, acquiring a monthly rent instead of a mortgage.

He lost all interest in the things he loved to do. He stopped calling his friends. When his mother called he tried to sound upbeat, but she could hear the change in his voice. When she asked, he just said that he was tired. Mothers know better though and she was determined to find out.

When Christian left, he only told his parents that he saw Jorge and got the money from him. They were somewhat relieved when they found out that Jorge would not be bothering them, since he would be in jail for a long time.

He went to the bank himself to care for the debts, and pay off the house in full. His parents would only have to contend with the bills they made from that point forward. Of course, they questioned how he managed to get the money from Jorge. He only assured them that they didn't need to worry themselves with the details, and that everything was under control. Inside though, he was angry with his brother for putting them and him in the existing situation. This anger carried over to mix with the depression, making it ten times worse.

When he entered the house, he put the bills and letters aside to open the package from New York. He removed the item from the box; it was a wooden tiger. He studied the intricate details, as he ran his fingers over its sleek design. There wasn't a note enclosed, so he turned the box over to see a return label with Elizabeth's name and address stamped upon it. Without wasting another moment, he picked up the phone and dialed her number.

Expecting to hear the familiar message on her machine, he almost hung up when he heard her answer.

"Elizabeth is that you," he reluctantly asked.

"Christian? I never thought I'd hear from you again," she answered with excitement in her voice.

"I've been trying to get in touch with you. Didn't you get my messages?"

"Yes, but when I tried to return them, there was a message that your phone had been disconnected."

"Oh. I'm sorry about that. I was in the process of moving at the time. I am settled, and the number is the same. How was China?"

"It was great! Did you get the package I sent to you?"

"Yes. That's why I'm calling. It's beautiful. Thank you. I have the perfect place on the mantelpiece for it."

"I'm glad you like it. You know, I can finally take some of my vacation time," Elizabeth hinted.

"That's great. I'm glad for you. You deserve it," he answered without taking the bait.

"I thought maybe we could get together unless of course, you have other plans," she replied, trying not to sound like she was intruding.

"Sure, that would be great," he said without much enthusiasm.

"Are you sure? I don't want to..."

He cut her off mid-sentence.

"No, I would like to see you again. Don't mind me; I've had so much on my mind lately. Seeing you again would be great. Can you fly out here, or did you want me to go there," he asked hoping that she would come out to him.

"Either is fine. Which is easier for you?"

"Well, if you don't mind coming out here; only because I'm still getting settled."

"No problem. What day do you want me to come, and can you meet me at the airport?"

"How about Friday, yes, once you get your arrival time, let me know and I'll be there."

"Then I'll see you on Friday. Good night Christian."

"Good night Elizabeth. Dulce suenos."

"What?"

"Sweet dreams."


Christian was waiting at the gate when Elizabeth arrived. They hugged, and then he walked her to the baggage claim area. She felt an air of coolness in his demeanor.

"Maybe I shouldn't have come," she thought to herself but wanted to say aloud.

On the way to his house, he let her know that he would be staying with friends and she could stay at his place. He would introduce them at dinner. After all, it wouldn't be right to have her stay with people she had just met for the first time. Elizabeth started to feel uncomfortable about the whole trip and wondered why he wanted her to come at all. She tried to make the best of the situation, however weird it might have seemed.

"There must be an explanation for the way he's acting," she thought.

They arrived at his apartment, and he carried her bags in. She followed him like a lost puppy, or so she felt. This was certainly not going the way she planned.

"Make yourself at home. Do you want a glass of wine," Christian asked as if he had just met her.

"Sure, that would be nice," she answered, hoping that it would have a calming effect on both of them.

He sat beside her on the couch, yet kept a considerable distance between them. At least he seemed less tense after awhile. He asked her about China, but never mentioned the rest of her trip in Venezuela. She stayed away from the subject too and waited for him to bring it up.

They met Diana and Carlos at the pizza parlor for "dinner." Diana was more talkative than her newly wedded husband of four months was. She and Elizabeth hit it off right from the start. Her bubbly personality set Elizabeth at ease.

Diana was already talking about taking her shopping while she was visiting. The guys on the other hand were content to talk about work. Christian wasn't into sports, so that left Carlos with little to add to the conversation.

After dinner was over, they went back to Christian's for the dessert, which Diana had so carefully prepared. Staying with the Italian theme, she made a tiramisu; ladyfingers soaked in coffee and rum, added to this was a Mascarpone cream mixture.

Garnished with shaved chocolate, it was a delight, which simply melted in their mouths.

"Did you remember to get the movie," Diana asked in between bites.

"Yes, I did. I have it right here," Carlos replied, taking the movie from the counter.

The movie ended up being long and boring, not to mention filled with subtitles. Elizabeth couldn't keep up with both the subtitles and the actions. Christian looked like he dozed off a couple of times.

Diana and Carlos were definitely into subtitled movies, although they talked through most of it. It was obvious they had seen it before, judging by the constant "Oh, watch what happens next," or "Pay attention, this is a good part."

When it was finally over, Elizabeth silently released a sigh of relief. While Diana and Carlos were still discussing the movie, Christian began cleaning up. Elizabeth volunteered to help.

"Sorry about the movie. I wasn't with them when they went to get it," Christian apologized.

"Don't worry about it. Christian, are you all right," she asked hesitatingly.

"I'm just tired, that's all. I'm sorry if I've been a bad host," he retorted as he placed the last plate in the dishwasher and walked out of the room.

Standing there alone in shock, Elizabeth decided that she would leave tomorrow unless things changed drastically. She went back out in the living room to find Christian and their guests already putting on their coats.

"It was nice meeting you Elizabeth. Don't forget to save a day for us to go shopping," Diana reminded her.

"Sounds like a plan Diana," Elizabeth answered, trying to sound excited about the venture.

"It was a pleasure to meet you Elizabeth," Carlos remarked.

Christian exchanged pleasantries with her as well and then kissed her on the cheek.

"I'll be over in the morning, around nine, if that's all right with you."

She had just about answered him when he departed, leaving her to find things for herself.

"What a welcome this has been so far," she thought to herself.

Elizabeth woke at seven, and got up to make breakfast. The phone rang and she decided to let the answering machine pick up.

"Elizabeth, this is Christian. Can you pick up?"

"Hello."

"Hi, sorry to call so early, but I'm not going to be able to meet you until later on. I have a job that I need to finish first."

"That's all right. I'm sure I can find things to do. Do you have any idea when you'll be done?"

"I can be done around four if I push it. I'll call before I leave the site, okay?"

"Sure, no problem, see you then."

"Thanks. Bye."

Disappointed once again, Elizabeth decided to go jogging to work out her frustration. She remembered when they were driving in yesterday, that the park wasn't far from there. It turned out to be only three blocks away. It was empty for such a beautiful morning, much different from the parks in New York. Her senses awakened to all the sights and sounds. She felt the warm sun on her face and reached upwards as if she could capture it. The birds sang around her, flying from one tree to another. She caught sight of two squirrels chasing each other before they disappeared into the underbrush.

After a considerably long jog, she stopped to sit on a bench and drink in the beauty around her. While sitting there, she noticed the opening of an art gallery across the street and went over to see what they had to offer.

One of the proprietors met her at the door as she entered and welcomed her to look around. There were many sculptures as well as paintings, both using several mediums. As in other galleries and museums, there would always be that intriguing piece that caught her eye. As she studied it carefully, the second proprietor came to inquire about her interest in the painting.

"May I help you with this painting, miss? It's called The Color of Dreams," he commented, as he walked toward her.

"Yes, as a matter of fact, you can," Elizabeth replied, as she turned to face him.

"Mark?"

"Elizabeth? How long has it been? Ten years?"

"I believe it's been more like fifteen years," she smiled.

"Well, the years have been good to you. Are you living here?"

"No, I'm visiting a friend while I'm on vacation."

From the backroom, the other owner called to remind him they needed to get set up for that evening.

"I'll be right there, Sandy. We're having a grand opening party. Why don't you and your friend join us tonight? Then we can catch up on what's happened in our lives since college."

"I don't know if he has anything planned, but I'll ask him. What time does it start?"

"The reception is at six-thirty. I hope you can come, Beth. It's been too long."

As Elizabeth left the gallery, she was so taken off guard with seeing Mark again that she forgot about the painting. The fact that he called her Beth struck something deep inside. So many thoughts were running through her mind. What were the chances of running into him here, after so many years? He's in quite a different career from the one he was pursuing in college. Hadn't she heard somewhere that he was married? What would Christian think about going tonight?

The last thing on Christian's mind was going to a black-tie affair. He had worked hard all day trying to finish the job that should have taken at least two more days. He would still have to go back tomorrow. At that point, he just wanted to take a hot shower and relax.

He told Elizabeth that she could go if she wanted, but he couldn't stand up any longer. She chose to stay with him so they could spend some quality time together. However, by eight, he was already beginning to doze off on the couch. Now, she had wished that she had gone by herself to the gallery.

The next day she went to apologize to Mark for not showing. Sandy let her know that he was out, but would be back shortly. In the meantime, Elizabeth went to look at the painting from the day before. Unfortunately, for her, it wore a sold tag.

Mark came in ten minutes later, and asked her to wait while he brought some packages in the back room. She was still looking at the painting when he returned.

"Don't worry about this," he said taking the sign off the painting.

"I only put it there so no one would buy it last night. I knew you were interested in it."

"Well, that was very thoughtful of you. As soon as I saw it, I pictured it in my apartment. Let me give you my credit card. Do you need my ID," she asked playfully.

"I need it for your address and so forth."

"I can give you that information without subjecting you to my wonderful glamour shot."

"Glamour shot? Now I have to see it," he said grinning like a Cheshire cat.

"I was being sarcastic, thank you very much."

"There you are, Miss. It is still Miss, isn't it?"

"Yes."

"Good, then you won't mind if I ask you to lunch?"

"Do you always ask your customers to have lunch with you?"

"I only ask those who have the name, Elizabeth Fitzgerald. So far, you are the only one. So, is it a yes?"

"Sure, that would be nice."

At the cafe, they talked about the things that had happened since the last time they were together. Neither of them had married, but both had come close. Mark had spent some time in Europe after college, where he developed his taste for fine art. Elizabeth had used photography for her creative expression. Both of their dads had passed away within the three years after they left college. Their sisters, who had been close friends, became nurses.

"I can't believe we ran into each other Beth. I've always wondered what happened to you after...well you know," he said without looking directly at her.

"After we broke up, it took me a while to recover, but I survived," she said sweetly.

"I wanted to call or write so many times but..."

"It's probably better that you didn't. Anyway, it's over. Let's just put the past behind us."

"And start over," he asked hesitantly.

"Start over? Mark, I can't do that right now. I'm in a relationship with someone."

"Oh, would that be with the friend that you're visiting?"

"Yes."

"Then why do you refer to him as just a friend?"

"Because, well it's just that, it's complicated."

"Beth, I know you better than that. I've seen you in love before. This isn't your look of love. You're not even sure of yourself when you talk about him. You're just playing it safe and hoping at the same time. Beth, please give us another chance. I promise it will be different," he pleaded as he leaned in closer and kissed her.

All the past emotions that she had for him came to the fore. She responded willingly to him until a voice from behind her made her shudder.

"So, this is what I mean to you Elizabeth. I asked if you could find something to do while I was at work. This isn't what I had in mind," Christian said trying to keep his voice down to avoid embarrassment.

"Christian, if you give me a chance, I'd like to introduce you to Mark Stevens, my friend from college who owns the art gallery," Elizabeth said nervously.

Mark stood up and held out his hand. Christian looked at him but refused.

"Hey Christian, I'm sorry. That was all me, not Beth. She told me about you but I pushed her. Don't take it out on her."

"Don't tell me what I can and cannot do. Elizabeth, I think it would be better if we discussed this alone. Are you coming or not," he asked, while walking out the door.

"Mark, I really should go. I'm sorry."

"No, I'm sorry. I shouldn't have put you in this situation. I've messed things up between us again. Look if you can forgive me, you know where I am, right?"

"I have to go, Mark," she said without looking into his eyes.

The walk back to the apartment was silent, but Christian made up for that when they were inside.

"Elizabeth, or should I say, Beth, why did you come here in the first place," he asked while pacing the floor.

"You know why I came, to be with you."

"That's funny because since you've been here we haven't spent much time together."

"And whose fault is that?"

"Look I have a job to do. I can't just walk away from it as easily as you can from yours," Christian remarked sarcastically.

"Easily, do you know what it took to get this time off? This was the time that I thought we were going to use to get to know one another more. But you've had an attitude since you picked me up at the airport, and you've found every excuse not to be with me besides," Elizabeth retorted.

"Attitude, well forgive me if I have things on my mind that I haven't shared with you. Maybe it wasn't such a good idea that you came here," he said facing the window.

He began playing with the chess pieces on the table below it.

"Checkmate," he said in a low but audible voice.

"Excuse me," Elizabeth asked confused.

"Checkmate. Do you know what it means exactly?" Before she could say anything, he answered the question for her.

"It's a combination of Persian and Arabic language meaning dead king," he commented, knocking over the king.

"Christian, what do you want me to do? I'll stay and work things out if you want me to or go if you don't."

"I don't know what I want," he answered softly.

"Well until you decide, I think I'm going to move into the hotel down the street."

When he didn't respond, she went into the bedroom to pack and call a taxi. After coming back out in the living room, she thought he would have something to say. He just kept standing and staring out the window, motionless and expressionless.

"I'm leaving Christian. You know where to reach me."

There still wasn't any reaction.

With tears in her eyes, she said good-bye, and walked out. However, she left for the airport instead of the hotel. He watched as she got into the taxi and drove away. His eyes filled up, as he realized what he'd lost by letting her go. However, he knew it was too late now to fix what he had ruined.

The flight home was not pleasant, for more than the obvious reason. There was turbulence from a thunderstorm, a little kid about four rows back wouldn't stop crying, and the older woman next to her had to keep getting up to use the facilities. Fortunately, she would be home in a couple of hours, or so she thought. The plane had to make a stop in Chicago and then there was a three-hour layover. By the time she returned to her seat on the plane, she was ready to lose her patience altogether.

When she arrived home, she dropped her bags on the floor, and fell on the bed. Fully dressed, she crawled under the covers and cried herself to sleep in only a matter of minutes.

The exhaustion took over, and brought with it not just a dream, but rather, it was a nightmare. It was cloudy, but she could see Christian in the distance, walking around as if he were blind. He stumbled from the shoulder into the road. As she watched, she saw an approaching car headed right for him. She tried to scream to warn him, but her voice stayed as a whisper. By the time her voice reached him, so had the car. It hit him even though it tried to swerve out of his path.

She watched as the driver got out of the car. Mark stood over him and called the passenger from the vehicle. She watched as she saw herself emerge from the car and run over to Christian. He was bleeding but conscience. She knelt and held him in her arms, thinking he would die at any moment. In a split second, he disappeared into thin air. She turned to find that Mark had disappeared too, along with the car.

Alone, the freezing rain started to pour down. She looked down at her hands, covered with several colors of paint. At that point, her strength drained from her. She curled up on the side of the road and tried to keep warm.

She was jolted back into consciousness by the phone ringing off the hook. By the time she became untangled from the sheet and comforter, the answering machine had picked up the call for her.

"Beth darling, it's your mother. Are you there? I'm in town for a couple of days and I thought we could get together. I'm staying at the Embassy. Call me, we'll do lunch."

"Great timing mother, how do you do it? You always manage to contact me when I'm at my worst. Then I have to listen to your constant complaining about whatever lawyer you're working with at the time. Why me? Why now," she asked, pulling the covers back over her head. Remembering the nightmare, she quickly thought better of going back to sleep and went to get something to eat instead.

Mark waited several days for Elizabeth to return. When she didn't, he had the painting mailed to her home address. She wondered what she had ordered as she signed for it. After checking the return address, she knew what was within the carefully wrapped package. Hanging it on the wall brought back the memories of the two men in her past. She stared at it carefully, examining more closely than she had at the gallery.

"The color of dreams, isn't that ironic?"

She thought about calling Mark to thank him but decided to send a note instead. In combing through her wallet for a stamp, she came across a piece of paper with his phone number on it. After mulling it over for a minute or two, she began dialing the numbers.

"Hello?"

"Mark?"

"Beth? Where are you? I've been trying to reach you for days now."

"I'm back in New York."

"New York, but why; I thought..."

"I had to leave right away."

"He didn't hurt you after you went with him, did he? Because if he did..."

"No, he's not like that. I decided it would be better if I came back home," Elizabeth sighed.

"Why didn't you come back to me? It will be different this time Beth. You can believe it or not, but I've changed since college. My life is finally in order. I've been sober for eight years now. The gallery, which I'm part owner of is bringing in more than enough money. We'd be all set financially. The only thing I want and need is you to share it with me. There'll be no more lies Beth. Just give me one chance to prove it to you, and I promise you won't regret it."

"Mark I don't know if I'm ready to do this again. My head is still spinning from everything that's happened."

"Beth, when I kissed you, I felt that love that we once had come flooding back. Look, I'm not asking for a miracle. Just let me show you. If it's not the life that you want, you can leave and I'll never try to contact you again."

"I'm going to have to think about it, Mark. I just don't know. I have too many emotions going on at one time. Besides, I wouldn't want you to be the rebound guy."

"Why don't you let me worry about that? Will you come?"

"Not yet. I have to set everything straight first, so I can figure things out logically. It might take me a while. Right now I don't know what all these feelings are going to lead to."

"Hopefully back to me. I'll wait for as long as it takes Beth. Search your feelings, but please save some of them for me."

They ended their conversation, and Elizabeth wondered which feelings; those from the past or the present that her heart would hold on to when it came to the final decision.


Christian, on the other hand, was trying desperately to get rid of the feelings of hatred he now had for his only brother. They used to be so close when he was there. Jorge even looked up to him once, and they had mutual respect for one another. Now, it was different. His brother was a changed person. He hadn't even given him a chance to say anything before disowning him. Then again, he may have already secretly done that when Christian moved out of the country.

He had never felt such intense emotions as these. Not even the love he had for Elizabeth could compare. He was angry at himself for having them and for shutting Elizabeth out when she was with him. Then he remembered the encounter in the cafe.

"What differences does it make anyway? I saw how she looked at him. That was more than a friendly kiss, and I didn't see her resisting. It doesn't matter. I don't care for her anymore. I was a fool to think that she would come to love me!"

As he ranted on, he took the wooden tiger that she had given him, and sent it flying across the room. It crashed against the bookcase and split into several pieces.

Angry with himself for the rage he had displayed, he leaned on the mantelpiece with his head in his hands. Frustrated he roughly ran them through his hair.

"Why? Everything is just falling apart around me and I don't know how to stop it! Diana's right. I am a time bomb ready to explode."

He didn't know how to diffuse it. Could he do it, before it was too late? Carlos and Diana tried to help him, but he would not budge to save face.

"Forget your pride brother and talk to me. It can't get any worse by telling me. We've been best friends for a long time now. Are you afraid I would think any less of you for it? You should know me better than that, Christian. I'll admit that I'm hurt that you can't share whatever it is that's eating you alive. If I were in that situation, you'd feel the same way. At least I thought you would, maybe I'm wrong."

"No, you're right Carlos. But it's not that simple."

"Try me."

After a while, Christian finally broke down and told him everything that had happened back home and what had happened with Elizabeth.

"Aye, aye, aye," was all Carlos could manage at first.

"Yeah, aye, aye, aye," Christian repeated.

"I don't know how you've kept this in so long."

"Trust me, it hasn't been easy. I've been going crazy for what, six months now?"

"Try a year Christian," Carlos answered sadly.

"A year, it can't be that long. I was only home in February."

"And what is the date today, my friend?"

Christian looked at his watch, for the days had run into one another, leaving him oblivious to the passing of time.

"January 25th. My god, where has the time disappeared to," Christian asked in disbelief.

"You've been in your world since you returned brother. We've been trying to tell you, but you just wouldn't listen."

"It's more like I didn't hear you. I blocked out everything and everyone."

"Including Elizabeth," Carlos added.

"Don't go there. I don't even want to start that conversation."

"But you didn't even explain it to her," Carlos argued.

"I'm telling you man, back off. Whatever we had, if anything, is gone, and I don't care to discuss it at this moment."

Christian made his point quite clear between his tone of voice and the stern look. Carlos took the warning and chose to change the subject, instead of chancing the wrath that would have befallen him if the conversation had continued.

"Hey, Diana's at her sister's house. Do you want to get something to eat? Shoot some pool?"

"I'm not very good company."

"It doesn't matter. Come on, you look like you need a night on the town," Carlos said as he slapped him on the back.

The blank page of the journal stared up at Elizabeth. She was going to start writing, but spent the good portion of an hour thinking about everything that had happened in the past year. She relived the years spent with Mark, the good and the bad, although the bad outweighed the good in that relationship. The endless questions with their inadequate answers controlled her thoughts. Did she want to take another chance on him? After all, he has been sober for eight years now, or so he said. Did she even love him anymore, certainly not the way she used to when they were in college? She had matured over the years. Had he matured? Was it just another game? She never liked his games. He always won and she, as the loser, would be left alone and hurting. Could someone change his personality and lifestyle to the degree, which he was suggesting? Maybe, but does that mean it will stay that way if we started over?

Her thoughts switched to Christian. What could she determine from that situation? First, he seemed to be prone to rage, as their first and last encounters showed. It didn't appear that it required much to set him on edge. How much did she honestly know about him? They didn't exactly spend that much time together in Venezuela. Granted, after the near-death experience, they hit it off and had two great days together. What did she know about his family or him for that matter? Was it just out of guilt that he showered her with kindness, or was there something from outset between them? What was the actual explanation for his disposition when she went to California? Would she ever have concrete answers to any of these confusing questions? She shook herself from the trance-like state, and looked down at the empty journal. She couldn't help but necessitate the concluding question aloud.

"How did my life get so complicated in such a short measure of time?"

Like characters in a play, we are drawn together, and then torn apart by the story-weaver.

Who chooses the outcome of our journey?

Are we able to break free from its grasp, and endure on our own merits?

Can we make life-long decisions for ourselves?

Is it conceivable to trust that we can cut the strings by which the puppeteer has us dangling precariously over potentially dangerous situations, and survive?

Why do they become tangled in a web of uncertainties?

What or who operates the merry-go-round that everyone wants to stop and get off from

Moreover, if we do, will we then spin out of control, now that we are not held down by its gravitational pull, which keeps us firmly planted to solid ground?

The artist paints with delicate soothing stokes.

When anguish is deep within him, his brush sweeps recklessly across the canvas, creating chaos, or is it a masterpiece?

Can a wanton existence ever possess stability?

Why? That is the absolute question, the writer scribbles.

Is there an answer?

Is it possible that there are many feasible explanations?

The mind races with great haste to find an acceptable response.

One must create within oneself a rationalized solution to this inquiry.

It is crucial to surviving in this illogical world, that we announce our permanence.


A puzzled look came upon Elizabeth's face when she read the words she had penned on the once unadorned page. Never had she written anything like this before. From where had this all come? Certainly, this was out of character for her. Was it a creative element residing inside her, that until now she was unaware of its existence? Maybe, but what did it all mean? For now, like her dreams, it would remain unsolved.


After a time, Christian had begun to regret his hasty actions towards Elizabeth. He wanted to ask her to return to him. Yet, his pride continued to get the better of him. The same pride hindered him from going back and attempting to reconcile with his brother.

He found himself being able to disregard the tense feelings, and immerse himself in his work throughout the day. However, they found a way to transcend into his thoughts by night, and cloud his dreams. He desperately needed to find comfort from the one woman who never doubted or questioned him. Why hadn't she come to him? Was it because he had begun to love another?

His voice called to her through the mist, which blinded him from seeing anything but his hand in front of his face, a voice so distraught that he awoke in a cold sweat.

On one of these chilling occasions, he resigned himself to the idea of having lost her along with Elizabeth forever. This turning point led him to relent, and compose a letter to Elizabeth. His one desire was to procure her forgiveness. He instantly dismissed the prospect of her granting him another chance from his mind.

A sensation of relief washed over him once he sent the letter, and then there was one of trepidation, as the waiting game began. Would time present itself as the healer of his wounds? An optimist would venture to say that the letter would arrive to find its recipient ready to forgive, so the couple would live happily ever after.

However, as time and circumstances would have it, this was not to be the case. Elizabeth had, only hours before, left the country on another long assignment. The envelope with its contents found itself interned in a cold plastic box, for an undetermined length of time, at a branch of the United States Post Office, in New York City.

Paris is beautiful in the springtime. The Eiffel Tower means more when two lovers embrace, in its shadow. Walking along the Seine River, hand in hand with one another, brings the beauty of France to a climax. Elizabeth spent her days taking photographs, while Mark visited art galleries and met with local artists. The Left

Bank Cafe was their meeting place for lunch at one. It was the cultural scene where great artists, writers, and eminent intellectuals consorted at one time. These included Ernest Hemingway and Jean-Paul Sartre.

Their conversation included a discussion about the famous locale, along with the success each had so far that day. They secured dinner reservations at one of the area's busiest bistros. True to its word, the bistro was certainly crowded when they arrived at eight.

The host promptly seated them, and recorded their order for hors d'oeuvre order. Elizabeth chose snails in garlic butter with a crumb topping. Mark decided on the frog legs, which were also drenched in garlic butter. For the main course, both of them enjoyed filet mignon with mixed vegetables and tiny potatoes. For dessert, Mark indulged in sugared crepes flamed in liqueur, while Elizabeth savored every morsel of an egg custard with caramel sauce.

"You won't believe the business deal I made after lunch today, Beth. We will be adding some wonderful pieces to the gallery. I think it's going to make a huge difference in our success this year, compared to last."

"That's great. I'm glad everything is going so well."

"I wanted to speak with you about a new part of the gallery. It's going to be all framed photographs. I would like to feature your work, if you feel disposed to grace our gallery with it."

"Are you serious, you want to sell my work? I don't know what to say, Mark," she replied, still holding her fork in mid-air.

"How about… yes? Of course, you'd have to be present for the public induction ceremony, possibly make a small speech, and mingle with the prospective buyers. Nothing major," he chuckled.

"Nothing major, huh? If all that is minor, I'd hate to see what you call a major event," she replied.

"Really though Beth, will you consider becoming part of the gallery? It would mean so much to me. Of course, it wouldn't hurt your career either. All you would have to do initially is submit the pictures and I'll take care of the framing and so forth. It would be a challenge but I'm sure you're up to it," Mark remarked confidently.

"Oh, you are? And what makes you so sure that I'm up to it?"

"Because you've always loved a challenge, couple that with your creativity, and you've designed a perfect match. Speaking of perfect matches, have you considered my other offer? We do make a perfect match Beth. We could be married right here in Paris. How much more romantic can you get?

Elizabeth became serious.

"You're right; you can't get much more romantic than that. However, I haven't come to any conclusion about a permanent relationship yet. As far as the gallery, I would love to have my work displayed there. I'm not so sure about the speech though. When it comes to speaking in front of crowds, I tend to freeze."

"Well, maybe we can forgo the speech. So, what's on the agenda for tomorrow?"

"I'm traveling to the medieval towns of Alsace and Lorraine. After clamoring over citadels, and traveling through the countryside on Wednesday, a relaxing spa will be well needed and deserved. Then I'll be ready to explore the Château du Haut-Kœnigsbourg by Friday."

"Are we still meeting in Colmar on Thursday as planned," he asked.

"Yes, Colmar is a good vantage point. What a coincidence too. I was looking over some history on it yesterday. They call it "Little Venice."

"Why is that a coincidence," Mark inquired.

"That's the meaning of...," she said stopping short.

"What is it the meaning of?"

"Nothing," she said as if it didn't matter.

"Nothing, Beth you started to say something. What was it?"

"Venezuela," she said with downcast eyes.

"Oh, well that's interesting that you have that reoccurring theme. Maybe we'll go to Venice, Italy someday. So are you ready to go," he said callously and started to rise from his chair.

"Mark, don't be like that. It was just a coincidence with the names."

"Come on Beth. As usual, you forget how well I know you. You could never hide anything from me. Your voice and the guilty look on your face give you away. I know who is on your mind. You always wear your heart on your sleeve."

"I do not. What if I am thinking of him, Christian, there I said it, are you happy?"

"Beth, I won't be happy until I can have you for my own. Until you get him out of your head that will never happen. I can't help being jealous of him. He didn't know what he had until he lost you. I know because the same thing happened to me. Look, I'm sorry. I didn't mean to get you upset. Forgive me," he pleaded with puppy-dog eyes.

"Yes. Let's just forget this conversation ever happened, okay?"

"Okay."

In Alsace, Elizabeth photographed the half-timbered houses with flower-clad balconies. These balconies, covered in beautiful colors of red, pink, and green, went clear to the roof. The villagers gladly smiled for her, while they enjoyed the view of the countryside from their windows. The quaint pastel-painted villages and sleepy vineyards made interesting subjects. The architecture was abundant in this enchanting medieval town, more than Elizabeth was able to capture on film.

The sun shone brightly and added character to the vista, casting shadows as it went behind the cotton-like clouds. Alsace is a fairly dry, warm climate, and it proved to be just that during her short stay. Much of the region's attraction has to do with its cuisine. As Alsace is famous for its wine, Lorraine's claim is beer. So who could visit this peaceful, yet fortified town without having a glass/bottle of it with a quiche Lorraine? Elizabeth would not waive this one tempting treat.

Satisfied, she made her way back out into the warmth of the noonday's sunlight. This allowed her to accomplish a great deal before returning to the hotel. When she retired to her room, she thought about Mark's offer. It would be a great shot in the arm to be able to sell her work. However, did she want to go as far as being married to him? After thinking about it and trying to decipher everything in her mind, she decided that when they met the following day she would give him her answer.

After all, he was much different from years past. She still loved him, didn't she? Of course, she did. Maybe she would call him tonight instead of waiting. Yes, that was a good idea, she felt. Sitting on the edge of the bed, she found his hotel number and called.

The desk manager informed her that Mark had checked out of the hotel only an hour before.

"Well I'll just have to tell him tomorrow," she thought."

The next day at lunch, she surprised him with her decision. Mark's eyes lit up. He couldn't believe what he was hearing. He took her hands in his and kissed them.

"You'll never regret this decision, Beth. I promise. Oh, you don't know what a happy man you've made me. I love you so much. I always have. Let's celebrate!"

By the end of the night, Elizabeth had convinced herself and Mark that he was the one for her. Had she really? They planned to marry in Paris the following weekend, before returning to the States.

Everything went well for the first few days, but by day four, Elizabeth's doubts began to arise. Maybe it was just cold feet, she thought, as she tried to justify her feelings. After all, we did plan this in haste. That evening she attempted to reason with Mark to postpone the nuptials until they could have their family and friends with them.

"We can redo the ceremony when we get back, for their benefit," he argued.

"That's not the same thing," Elizabeth counter-argued.

By the time all the arguing and counter arguing finished, they were at odds with each other. Elizabeth accused him of rushing her so that she wouldn't change her mind, and he felt that she was just trying to back out altogether. At this point, they decided not to decide and went to their separate hotel rooms.

Attempting to distract herself from the chaos Mark managed to bring back into her life; she took out the laptop and checked her e-mail. One of the messages was from Stephanie.

It read this way:

'Elizabeth, a phone call came for you yesterday. It was from a Diana Montoya. She said that your friend Christian had to go back to Venezuela for his brother's funeral. She thought you might want to know. Her phone number is *** *** **** if you need to contact her. See you soon, Stephanie.'

Without hesitation, she called Diana. At this point, Diana proceeded to explain the whys and wherefores of Christian's behavior.

"If you just give him another chance Elizabeth, I know it will work out. He even confided in Carlos that he wrote to you to apologize, but you never responded."

"He did? When? I never received any letter from him."

"It was only within the past few weeks, I would imagine."

"I've been in Paris. That's where I am right now. And as of this morning, I was planning my wedding."

"You were planning your wedding? Congratulations! Oh Elizabeth, if I had known I wouldn't have suggested that you give Christian another chance. I'm sorry."

"Don't be sorry Diana. Things aren't going as well as I planned anyway. I'm so confused. I thought I loved Mark, but now I'm not sure. Maybe I need to settle things with Christian before I can go on. Do you have his family's address?"

Almost at the same moment that she ended the conversation with Diana, there was a knock on the door.

"Beth, can we talk please," Mark asked through the locked door.

Elizabeth opened the door.

"Mark, come in, we need to talk."

"Beth I'm sorry. I've been a fool to try to rush you into this marriage. I'm just so afraid that I'm going to lose you again, and I can't bear that thought."

"Mark, before you say anything else, I have to be honest with you. I thought that I could make myself love you again, but it's no use," she said as her eyes filled with tears.

"Beth it's just because I've been rushing you. Please take some time and rethink your decision. We don't have to get married right away. I thought getting married in Paris would be romantic, but we can do it wherever and whenever you want. Please reconsider Beth. I don't want to live my life without you," he said taking her hands in his.

"Mark, it's not you, it's me. I haven't been fair to either of us. I still have feelings for Christian, whether or not he still has them for me, I'm not sure. Either way, I'm going to Venezuela to find out. Christian's brother died, so I'm flying out on Saturday. I'm truly sorry Mark. I did try to rekindle my feelings for you. It's just not meant to be."

"Well I guess you did warn me about being the rebound guy, didn't you? I hope things work out for you Beth. I want you to be happy. You deserve it. If things don't pan out, you know where to find me. I'll always be there for you," he said as he kissed her for what he knew would be the last time.

Elizabeth hailed a taxi at the airport and headed straight for Christian's house. With only a basic understanding of Spanish, she wondered how she would communicate with his family if Christian weren't there. She retrieved her luggage from the trunk of the taxi, and paid the driver. Her nervousness became more obvious as she walked up to the door and rang the bell. The door opened, revealing a man with disheveled hair, and a three-day-old beard.

"Hola, Senor. Me llamas…," was all she managed to say before he interrupted her.

"Elizabeth? What are you doing here? How did you know," he cried.

Looking into his eyes, she asked, "Christian? I…I didn't recognize you."

Running his hand across his face and through his hair, he stammered, "Oh, I'm sorry, I must look disgraceful. I can fix it though. Please come in. Let me take your bags. I can't believe you're here! My family isn't here right now, but they will return soon. Here, sit down. Let me go and clean myself up."

Before he had a chance to get away from her, she called out to him.

"Christian, stop for a minute. Come here. Let me look at you."

He came and stood before her. She raised her hand and repeated the motions, which he had performed moments earlier. She ran her fingers through his hair, then across his beard, before holding his face within her slender hands. Her touch and consoling look pierced his heart.

"If you still want me, Christian, I'm here to stay."

All his emotions came flooding forth. He took her in his arms and kissed her passionately. He held onto her so tightly, as if she would disappear if he loosened his grip in the least. Was it the thought that he might just be dreaming that she was there before him.

DREAMING ---- he had dreamed that she would return to him. Now, the elusive woman in his dreams had become tangible, the one he could hold forever.

What about Elizabeth's dream? She knew the one she had been calling and searching for in her dreams. Now he was here, standing before her, lost in her eyes and within her touch, always.

# Thumbprints in the Stream of Time

It was the summer of 1979. I had just turned nineteen, and my education as an undergraduate, in the discipline of Archaeology, had only begun the previous September. A major in archaeology consisted of fourteen courses, including three units of independent studies.

Majors, who intend to engage in an excavation, as a significant component of their careers, are encouraged to participate in an archaeological field school, before the senior year. Being one of the students chosen to participate in an actual excavation, was more than I could have hoped.

Ancient history was always my favorite subject, but working to uncover it, coupled with an introduction to geology and anthropology, made a huge impression on my life. The experience of taking part in an actual excavation was the primary step in fulfilling the purpose of expanding my horizons; the first of which would be in Arizona.

Workdays were demanding and full. However, the joys of discoveries, and the splendors of the expedition's unspoiled desert canyon, exhilarated us. Yet, some of the things I encountered that summer proved absence in the "job description." For better or worse, they made me who I am today. It was an unforgettable journey into recreating not only the history of a Native American tribe, but in finding my true self. Before I get ahead of myself, let me take you back to a time when my life as an archaeologist was just beginning.

The list of classes needed seemed endless; the syllabuses list was even longer. With having a combination of archaeology, anthropology, and the study of Native Americans, the many lectures, papers, and lab work stacked up into a never-ending mountain of work. Although I enjoyed all the research, reading, and learning of lab techniques, I was longing to get my hands dirty in the trenches, or "squares" in this instance. Fieldwork!

It's amazing, as you go along you come to realize how much you don't know. Things thought to be "facts," turn out to be mere misconceptions and stereotypes of the "real McCoy." These needed quick dispelling in order for us to forge ahead.

As we began to develop a greater appreciation for Native Americans, we eventually saw the need to improve our cross-cultural communication and relationships, in theory. We didn't necessarily think the opportunity to put these skills into use would arise.

There is an assumption taken over the years, that the Hollywood versions of 'Pocahontas' and 'The Indian in the Cupboard' are the true versions of these people. Misconceptions that all Native Americans live in teepees, are a dying race, resemble war-whooping feathered and painted enemies, and are unprincipled heathen prove false. Until, one seriously takes the time to consider these, he/she only wallows in their ignorance. This proved once again, that ignorance isn't always bliss.

Thought provoking is a quote from Dr. Richard West Jr., who is a Cheyenne, and the Director of the National Museum of the American Indian. He said, "Not long ago, I went into a bookstore and asked the sales clerk for help in finding a particular book about American Indians. Believe it or not, he referred me to the nature section! It's as if we Native Americans were considered to be something less than human - something apart from the family of man. By the same token, it was not unusual when I was a child to walk into the museum and find Indians displayed next to dinosaurs and mammoths - as if we too were extinct."

It is a sad and sobering thought indeed for all to consider. Just travel to see and experience that they, as are other Native American tribes in this country, very much alive!

After much realization and consideration, the entrance into the intensive training of field school, that we yearned for all school year, was finally upon us.

We arrived in safari jeeps at the excavation site, and were anxious to start our expedition. First things first, the unpacking, and setting up of our site had to be accomplished, before any serious digging could occur.

Heavy knapsacks and duffle bags weighed us down with all the needed clothes and equipment, which were required. Some of the items found were an alarm clocks, flashlights, and extra batteries, cameras and film, matches, bottles of sunscreen, jackknifes, regional guidebooks, reading material, notebooks, sketchbooks, pens and pencils, and water bottles (just to name a few).

We chose our garments carefully. Included in this category of stout clothing were boots high enough to protect the feet and lower legs from snakes, sunglasses, hats, and plenty of bandanas.

We found the field conditions interesting. All of us slept in large canvas tents, with light bed frames and mattresses, complete with our sleeping bags. There was a nearby cabin with electricity, two full bathrooms, and an outdoor shower.

Speaking of showers, exfoliating the dirt found everywhere was a challenge. One soon realized, the shorter your hair and fingernails were, the better. My hair had never seen so much grit, sweat, pollen, and unfortunately dead insects. Forget the bubble baths for a while, at least until we were able to spend some time outside of camp.

There was a kitchen where we students prepared our breakfasts and lunches. We had our already-prepared dinners in an old adobe ranch house, which was just a short walk from camp.

We used the main tent for meetings of the minds, and thankfully protection from the elements, securely tied in place at the center of the excavation site. It was completely equipped with an artifact table, two computers, and our tools and supplies, the list of which follows:

Several sizes of mason's trowels
Small camp axes
Short handled hoes
Cloth gloves
Whisk brushes
Paintbrushes
Rulers
Measuring tapes
Levels
Drawing frames
Paper and cloth bags
Compasses
First aid kit (bandages, disinfectants, and ointments)
Snakebite kit

Other indispensable items included a rag saturated with kerosene to clean the measuring tape and prevent it from rusting, and a small supply of celluloid-acetone solution, to clean and preserve artifacts, and strengthen a fragile artifact or fragment of clay pottery, before removal from the dirt.

Part of the expedition was learning how to find the right place for an excavation or a dig site. The next step, survey, and grid out the area for dissection and corded into many squares.

The large wood-framed screens were set up to sift all of the dirt removed from the squares, to make sure no small artifacts or fragments escaped our notice. Dry land excavation techniques can often miss these most important samples. Therefore, a flotation device recovered any samples hidden within the dirt. As the dirt sinks to the bottom of the device, seeds, plant remains, charcoal, and bone float to the top, skimmed off, and set out to dry.

It's hard to describe to someone who doesn't have this appreciation, what it means to get right in there and dig with your hands. The feel of dirt in your hands and the smell of wet dirt, not mud, are exhilarating. Most people look at you as if you had two heads, rightly so, I guess if they've never really had the opportunity to experience it in this manner.

The first day, everyone is anxious to begin. Along with the surveying, there are trenches and postholes to dig, screens and other equipment strategically placed for maximum access, and mobility.

You start to get into the swing of things by putting all your energy, along with your back, legs, and arms into it. Trying to find a "comfortable" position when you do get to sit down at a square to begin digging is interesting. Getting the grip on the trowel, shovel, or just on the dirt itself, makes you feel like a kid. It's like going home again.

Professor Perry laid out the rules from the beginning.

"Number One - You and the shovel (trowel) need to become one. It has to be part of you, an appendage if you will. This is the best way to become an accomplished archaeologist. Well, it gets you started on your way anyhow.

"Now the day after, well your feelings, both mental and physical tend to shift. Waking up that first morning, sends shock waves through your body, as you try to exert enough energy to sit up on your bed. As you carefully put your feet on the floor, you find that muscles are throbbing in places where you didn't know muscles existed. However, after the initial shock begins to wear off, you shuffle to the shower, and wish you could have soaked in Epsom salt the night before.

"Discovering the bruises, cuts, and calluses is next. You feel like a war casualty. This is where the mental shock waves enter. 'What have I done? How long before my poor body gets used to this torture? Why am I doing this again?' Reality sets in, and the reasons why resurface, and reassure you that everything is going to be all right.

"The first couple of days are the worst though, as your body tries desperately to adjust to the rigorous life of a field school participant. As the weeks continue, the soreness wears away and the building of former flabby muscles begins to take shape. Sweating off a few pounds too is always encouraging. This is just the beginning. The best is yet to come."

This "pep talk" left some of us wondering if we were going to survive.

When you're excavating you stop many times and think, "Wow, there used to be people living here on the exact spot where I am right now." We encounter the past constantly while uncovering it. We touch cooking, war, and ceremonial implements, which were used by other human beings, possibly hundreds of years prior. In doing so, we lay bare history and the people whose lives encompassed it.

We extrapolate important and useful information from the objects left behind. By using careful techniques, it is possible to preserve the past and use it to help shape our future, if we allow it to do so. We've learned so much, but there is still out there waiting for discovery and understanding. It is an archaeologist's job to use every avenue given, in hopes of finding and uncovering as much of the past as humanly possible without destroying it.

When we found artifacts the square holes, we carefully brushed them to remove the surrounding dirt, triangulated, photographed, and drawn in its place before lifting it from its former home. Only then could it be tagged with its identification, measurements of depth, width, height, and length, name of the said square it came from, and its triangulated position, date found, and of course the name of the amateur archaeologist who worked so meticulously to unearth it.

Being a stickler for accuracy, I remember pouring over all of the records making sure everything coincided. The list of forms seemed endless. The survey maps and records were among the first we completed, along with the site excavation records. Then, of course, there were the daily field reports. We made sure the drawings on the grids of these reports matched the identification tags on the artifacts, so there would be no question in the future. If there was a feature, such as a hearth or anything made by the occupants, other than their tools or weapons, which was encountered, these were designated a place on the feature records. The stratigraphy records were important as well, in helping to piece the past together to make a clear picture. These reports were complete with sketches of the squares.

Each artifact uncovered had its individual record card, besides its entry in our field notebook. We recorded the triangulated measurements along with the measurements of the artifact and any identifying marks. We placed each artifact in individual paper bags, along with their ID tags, and assigned each one a number. The report would also list the square it belonged to, and if it came from within a feature, the feature number would be included. We recorded every minute detail in the field catalog. Duplicate records proved to be very helpful, should there be any loss or damage to an artifact record card.

We took photos of artifacts in situ (in the place where they were found), as well as features, thus providing a permanent record of all archaeological finds. Artifact markers, square and feature numbers, orientation arrows, and identification marks all appeared within the field of the camera. The one thing that always bothered me was how we took the artifacts instead of leaving them there for others to see and enjoy. They should be in a natural museum rather than a fabricated building. However, it wasn't my place to decide their fate.

I was glad not to be the only woman at the excavation. The six others ranged in age from 19-45, the oldest being Professor Jean Perry, who became a mom as well as a mentor to us. Thankfully, as we worked our way into a new decade, women were being able to represent the field as archaeologists, instead of archaeologists' wives. Our contributions were much more valuable than those of the early days were. We have more to give than just being an avocational archaeologist or the resident pot-washer.

Sophie Schliemann, although not well represented in history, was a pioneer for a woman's role in the world of archaeology. She stood beside her husband in the excavating work of what they believed to be the lost city of Troy. (Irving Stone: The Greek Treasure (1975)

Some of the masculine gender would emphatically argue that excavating is "man's work," (including some on the site) but we soon proved them wrong. Not being a stranger to hard work, we measured up quite well to the men, both in the field, and academically.

One of the two male professors was Evan Carter. He had also been one of my professors for two semesters during the academic year, so we knew one another by the time of the excavation.

Seven years my senior and measuring in at 6'2, he proved to be a rugged outdoorsman. He had dark brown hair and eyes, and donned wire-framed glasses. His beard covered a scar that ran the length of his left cheek, one he acquired from a bicycling accident years before.

He fit the typical stereotype of the Indiana Jones archaeologist. (Not that I'm complaining by any means.) Although he didn't carry a gun or a whip, his eight-inch divers' knife served him well. Everyone had a healthy respect for him.

We worked together closely, as he took an interest in my abilities as an aspiring archaeologist. We spent many hours talking about the excavation, the research aspect of the Navajo tribe, further education, family, goals, and oddly enough literature.

On the subject of literature, one of my favorite American authors is Henry David Thoreau. I longed at that time to visit Walden Pond, where he affectionately wrote about his home and its solitude there in Concord, Massachusetts. I have since visited this beautiful place several times in the last few years, and found it to be as delightful as he once described it. He made a statement regarding time that is worth quoting.

"Time will soon destroy the works of famous painters and sculptors, but the Indian arrowhead will balk his efforts and eternity will have to come to his aid. They are not fossil bones, but, as it were, fossil thoughts, forever reminding me of the mind that shaped them ... Myriads of arrow points lie sleeping in the skin of the revolving earth ... the footprint, the mind-print of the oldest men."

Evan's comment to this was, "Who could find fault with that statement?"

Undoubtedly, I concurred.

Evan sought to refine himself as an erudite professor, yet he never flaunted his intelligence, he only shared it intending to increase ours. He always had a stack of books to read, some scholastic some fictional. Many times, he burned the midnight oil into the wee hours of the morning, leaving his eyes were worn and tired. It was unfathomable how he functioned on so little sleep. I can only assume he had become accustomed to it over the years. I, on the other hand, was usually so worn out from the physical activities during the daylight hours that the dark proved to be a welcome retreat.

Being that it was summer in Arizona, there were many scorching hot days at the site, coupled with the slow painstaking work of excavating, writing reports, taking photographs, drawing sketches, and identifying and cataloging artifacts. As the desert sun rose higher in the sky, the air became drier which made it harder to breathe at times. The dust, which tended to fill our noses and lungs, contributed to the dilemma. Placing wet bandanas over our noses and mouths, served to alleviate ingesting some of the dirt. This left some, if not all of us, cranky at times (and at the most inopportune times too, I might add). When tempers flared, mediation took place between the parties involved. Everyone was grateful for the weekends. They were a welcome diversion from work and each other.

Recreation found its place too. The famous water fights took place often to cool off under the blazing white heat of the sun. One couldn't tell where the perspiration stains ended and the water stains began. The noon air might have been stagnant, but we refused to let its intensity conquer us. Sunburned and blistered, the days proved to be long at times. Many days we saw only a phantom rain, which did nothing to temper the desert aura that hung lazily around us. Despite this, many fauna and flora thrived in this setting.

Although rewarding, fieldwork brings with it a heavy price. Carrying the substantial buckets of dry earth wreak havoc on the back and arm muscles. Carpel tunnel syndrome creeps into the wrists and elbows, and restrictive sitting positions wear out the knees.

Nevertheless, given the opportunity to reconstruct history, outweighs the many aches and pains that it bestows upon those who chose to embrace it. Looking back, after two decades though, my body doesn't quite agree with me.

The sifted piles of soil grew rapidly, as the screens were constantly in motion, always ready to reveal an elusive shard, pieces of flint or bone.

We paired up for the excavation. Sheila and I worked together at first, but not by choice. It wasn't a good match for either of us, and we both knew it. She quickly volunteered for the "easier" tasks. By the end of the first day, she had inundated me with all the information she could think of about her wonderful life as "daddy's little girl."

"I'm just biding my time at school at his expense. I'm planning on eloping with my boyfriend."

"That's great," was all I managed to say before she started in again.

"And of course daddy will foot the bill for our honeymoon to Egypt because he loves me. He'll do anything I ask him too, watch him, and see if he doesn't."

It was beyond my comprehension why he would, but then what did I know about anything. After all, she knew so much more, being at the "mature age" of twenty-one. At any rate, she commandeered the entire conversation. I never got a word in edgewise, or as my drama teacher would say "an edge in word-wise." Imagining what her boyfriend of three months was like, I truly felt sorry for him.

Thankfully, after only three days we separated and paired off with two of the other girls. Ann was my new co-worker, and a quiet one at that. She and Sheila were like night and day. It was more like pulling teeth to get her to converse. At least the quiet was better than the constant chatter I had experienced in the days prior. Eventually, Ann opened up, and we soon became close friends.

We shared both fun and hair-raising experiences that summer. For instance, we were all out driving on the mountainous roads, when we came upon one, washed out from a previous storm. We began backing up to turn around. Thank goodness, we were going at a snail's pace, to accomplish this. We went too far back, and began sliding off the three-foot overhang. The van leaned precariously above the jagged and merciless rocks below.

"We're going to die," Sheila shouted.

"We're not going to die. Just sit still. Don't make any sudden moves," Professor Perry answered.

The sweat was thick on Evan's face and neck as he carefully tried to rectify the situation.

Our lives literally "hung in the balance" at this point. I held my breath, and unknowingly dug my fingernails into Ann's arm. She didn't realize it either at the time.

"We're going to die," Sheila screamed again and then proceeded to ramble in French.

It was the strangest thing. Evan's patience was tested and quickly became expended. He answered her terrified outbursts in a manner we thought he was incapable of, until then.

His voice thundered, "If you say another word you will."

It made the hair on our necks stand up and take notice. We hoped he was referring to the fact that we would die only if he couldn't concentrate on what he was doing. Sheila didn't utter another sound nor did anyone else.

Refusing to yield to the gravitational pull, we miraculously avoided death's grip, for yet another day.

Ann and I were soon termed "instigators," for the harmless pranks we pulled. The "lemon meringue pie incident" became our first and most famous mission together, as partners in crime.

As I recall, Charles and Evan had been harassing us all day. So of course, revenge was in order. It was a Friday, meaning we could spend the weekend off-site. The four of us drove into the city that evening. We had dinner, and went to the hotel to unpack. In our room, Ann and I conspired to get the guys back for all the "abuse" we took during the day.

We threw several ideas on the table, but the lemon meringue pie seemed to be the best one. From that moment on, we would seek out the best time to purchase and conceal the pies, until the perfect moment.

Charles and Ann had been dating since the beginning of the previous school year, and their relationship was stable enough to withstand a prank or two. After all, Charles was a fun person with a wonderful and understanding personality. He could both take and dish out the jokes. He was always coming up with "outside the norm," as he put it, ideas that would make us laugh until our sides hurt. He was a sweet guy, who knew how to treat a girl right.

The question for me was how would Evan react? Would he see it as a childish antic or join in on the fun? The mystery was soon to be uncovered.

The following morning, the guys went shopping for new boots, while Ann and I visited a nearby bakery, to get the needed supplies for our picnic. The anticipation was building, making it even more difficult to contain ourselves. Somehow, we managed to do so, until lunchtime in the park.

Knowing things would get messy, to say the least, we both brought towels (wet and dry) and put them in our backpacks the night before. Apparently, we thought this measure of preparation would suffice, since we hadn't brought anything else to assist in combating the inevitable.

We finished our sandwiches, and as calmly as we could, we offered dessert. Our hands were shaking, as we removed the pies from the boxes, and all but dropped them on the guys. After the initial shock, they picked up some of the remaining pie, and threw it back at us. Meringue flew everywhere, and of course, smearing us with it wasn't good enough for them. They had to do one better, by adding a healthy portion of dirt and grass to the mixture, and then kindly rubbing it into our hair, and across the back of our necks.

It was very difficult to free ourselves from their grasp, and try to escape further retaliation. Ann, having been on the track team, could outrun us all. She took off on a hundred-yard dash. She managed to hide among the trees before Chuck caught her. He was running right by the spot where she stood, when Ann, thinking he saw her, let out a scream. Had she not exposed her hiding place, she would have been safe. Charles stopped short in his tracks and spun around. Since she was still frozen, he had time to grab her around the waist, and carry her back, kicking and screaming. Thankfully, there were only a few people in the park. They seemed to be amused at our display of tomfoolery.

It was a good thing we weren't too far from the hotel, as the towels didn't prove to be of much help. The looks we received, as we walked by the front desk, were interesting. I'll venture to say they never had guests like us, before or after our stay with them. This day, would be the first of many extraordinary ones spent together.

All the sights, sounds, tastes, and feelings of the desert life heightened our senses. That experience will always remain deep within me. Even now, the smell of burning mesquite brings back memories of those summer nights under the full moon, with the coyotes howling from the mountaintops. Their sounds were haunting, and sometimes frightening, if they seemed to come too close to the camp, as they called each other in a frenzied tone of voice, warning of impending danger.

Remembering, as if it were yesterday, was the first thunderstorm Evan and I saw in the desert. We were driving back to the site, after one of our frequent trips into town for food supplies.

The sky darkened quickly, as the storm rolled in. Birds of prey and others scattered quickly, seeking protection from the inevitable. The heavens opened, and sent forth millions of pelting raindrops to the dry, cracked earth. The thunder roared like a freight train. We watched the spectacular display of creation in tremendous awe, from our refuge in a nearby cave. As I turned to comment on the storm's magnificent power, Evan was already facing me. Before any words issued forth from my lips, his were descending upon them. The feelings created were as electrifying as the lightning, which ripped through the nebulous sky, and singed the air around us.

I stood speechless afterward, either out of my weakened condition or of sheer surprise.

Two weeks later, Evan and I went to visit some good friends of mine, Amber and Robert Shea. They hadn't seen me since high school so they were ecstatic to have us. While grilling steaks, the guys quickly became friends. Amber and I filled one another in on what had been happening in our lives, while tossing salad and preparing a scrumptious dessert.

"Now that the guys are out of earshot, tell me. What's going on with you and ... Dr. Carter," she giggled, and rolled her eyes.

"Well, it's all very new actually. It started a couple of weeks ago when we were in a cave."

"You were in a cave?"

"We were waiting out the thunderstorm when he turned and kissed me."

"Oh, that's so romantic. I've got goose bumps just thinking about it. Then what," she asked, as she moved in closer.

"Then... nothing; the storm stopped, we got in the jeep and drove back to the site," I said nonchalantly.

A disappointing look came into her eyes. "Nothing, one kiss and that was it? I mean you didn't even say anything to each other after that?"

"We never said anything about the kiss. I was so taken back I didn't know what to say. I hadn't expected him to do that. I didn't know he felt that way about me. It took him a couple of days to mention anything about it."

"And …?"

"And he said that he cared for me. We have a wonderful time together, especially with Ann and Charles. You'll have to meet them."

As I told her the story of the infamous pie incident, she was practically on the floor in stitches. She lost it when I remarked, "Maybe it's because he's older and more reserved, but I have great respect for him. He's not, well you know, immature," I laughed.

Just then, Robert and Evan walked in through the patio door, only to find us laughing hysterically. The tears were streaming down our faces.

"What's so funny," Robert asked.

"Yeah, let us in. We could use a good joke," Evan added.

"It's just girl talk, you wouldn't appreciate it," Amber choked.

"I'm sure you had your "guy talk" out there too," I replied while reaching for the tissue box.

"Us," they both said and gave one another a dumbfounded look.

"Nah, not us."

We all cracked up at that point.

Trying to compose herself Amber inquired, "So how are the steaks coming?"

"All set, just waiting on you girls."

"We're ready if you can help us carry some of these things outside," she said winking at me behind Evan's back.

Storytelling and laughter accompanied dinner. I learned so much about Evan that night.

While sitting on the deck and enjoying several glasses of wine with our friends, we watched the evening hours fade away. Not wanting to leave, I pictured what our life would be like if we settled here. Then the realization of my archaeological career took precedent. Not wanting to give this up either, dreams of being married and settling down would have to take second place for a while at least.

The weeks that followed proved to be fruitful, as far as the dig was concerned. Working diligently, we uncovered a fire pit with charcoaled edges. There were stones inside the circle called potboilers. They serve the purpose of heating the pots faster when placed within them. We also found several beautiful obsidian points within the pit. They are not arrowheads or spearheads unless you find them attached to an arrow or a spear. They were well-made tools, to say the least. The fine precision these points have for cutting is amazing. They slice through leather as if it were butter, extremely sharp! We also found several stone axes, and a mortar and pestle set, used to grind corn.

The extra care we gave to uncovering the hearth was all for naught, when one night it was completely ruined. Awoken from deep sleep around 4 a.m., we heard the roar of several engines. As we flew out of the cabins and threw on the searchlights, we saw three dirt bikes speeding away. Hours later, when we assessed the damage, we found the hearth, and a few other squares destroyed from the vandals spinning their tires in them.

Evan alerted the police, and they offered to put an officer on guard overnight at the dig site. Thankfully, we didn't need him to exercise his law-enforcing powers, as the vandals never returned. Nevertheless, the loss of valuable information and artifacts had been lost.

The following weekend, Evan and I went hiking. Not far from the excavation site, we came across a cave. It was there, we saw at least one of the dirt bikes at the entrance. Evan prepared his diver's knife. Afraid, but needing protection from whatever we were going to encounter, I followed him. Carefully we crept around to the cave's opening, and there they were.

Not the culprits mind you, but two scantly clothed lovers instead. They looked up in embarrassment. As the young man looked away, the girl's eyes met Evan's, and I saw her surprised look appear.

"Evan?"

"Lianne?"

Now, the embarrassment was becoming contagious. I turned away so as not to complicate matters.

Evan tactfully explained why he thought they were the ones who damaged our site with dirt bikes, and apologized for intruding. She assured Evan that she forgave the intrusion and accusations, and then dared to end the conversation with "Nice seeing you again, Evan." This was much to the dismay of her boyfriend, who wasn't pleased at all.

We left in haste, and I muffled a laugh, until we were out of earshot.

"Old girlfriend," I inquired.

"Not quite, although she'd like to think so. I know her parents. They're good friends of mine. Let's just say, she's always been the wild one in that family, and leave it at that."

"Whatever you say, boss," I chuckled.

David Hurst Thomas tells us why an entire site should never totally be unearthed. He said, "The idea is to leave parts of our sites unexcavated, as a legacy for our archaeological grandchildren, who doubtless will possess technology we cannot even imagine."

It was exciting to recreate ancient people's lifestyles. How each artifact fit like a piece to a puzzle was amazing. Nevertheless, one of the most challenging tasks for an archaeologist is to know how to interpret these artifacts into understandable human terms. In other words, reconstruct the lives of the people who left the remains.

Archaeology is a total study. It involves analyzing everything that remains from the past. This takes into account not only history, but science also. As we place the hat of a scientist upon our heads, we must collect the data or evidence, conduct experiments, formulate and test our hypothesis, and make logical conclusions. In doing this, we must transport ourselves back in time, and relive the lives of the people whose remains we hold gingerly within our grasp. The hope is that one can truly understand the people and their culture, clearly and concisely.

The conundrum of my life hadn't been as clear until then, or so I thought. I never really fit in anywhere, until I chose to pursue a career in archaeology, specifically studying Native American tribes. The more we learned about their culture and way of life, the more I felt drawn to these people.

Writing letters back home, proved to be the answer to the questions I had for a long time. My parents had always been supportive of the decisions I made. They were always there with advice to help me through the various stages of growing up, and I accepted it, for the most part because of the great love and respect I had for them. However, after writing and telling them of my experience and feelings of comfort for the first time in my life, nothing could have prepared me for the information that a visit from them revealed.

On one of the weekends, I met them in the city. We went to dinner, where they both seemed a little tired or preoccupied, but I dismissed it thinking it was due to the long ride there. When they said that they weren't tired I wondered, "What then?"

On arriving at the hotel, they invited me to their room to talk. My parents looked at one another, as if to ask which one of them would speak first. I understandable became nervous.

"Mom, Dad, what's going on? You look like you have something important to tell me."

"We do honey," my father said.

"We just don't know how to tell you though," mother added.

Now the thoughts were running through my head at great speed.

"What? Did someone die?"

"Vickie, you know we love you,"

"Please don't tell me you're getting divorced," I cut in, before she had a chance to finish.

"No, no," they both answered.

"Your father and I are so proud of you. You continue to amaze us with your driving force and accomplishments. We both love you very much. Because of our love for you, and the sentiments that you expressed in your last letter for the people you are studying, we feel that the time has come to tell you something, that you may or may not be ready to hear."

"Mom, I'm not following you."

"The reason for your strong attachment to these people is in part because we adopted you at an early age."

"You did what?"

"We knew the time would come when we would tell you, but didn't know that time would be now."

"Adopted?"

My chest tightened, making it hard to breathe. I felt frozen in time. Everything I had ever known came crumbling down around me."

"Yes," my father said.

"But I don't understand. What happened to my birth parents? Did they abandon me? Not want me?"

"Victoria, your parents loved you very much. They asked that when the time was right, we tell you about them. This seemed the right time."

"What we're going to tell you could open up a whole new outlook on life for you. I just hope you don't hold it against us for keeping this from you for so long."

"You see, your mother was Spanish-American, born and raised in Arizona and your father was Native-American from the Navajo tribe. They were good friends of ours.

Soon after you were born, they discovered that both of them contracted a respiratory disease. After two years, it had worsened dramatically. They died within weeks of one another. Their final wish was for your father and me to take you into our home, and care for you as if you were our own. All they asked is that when you wanted to know your heritage, we would present it to you. Your father and I agreed that this was the appropriate time, with you being so close to your real family."

I sat motionless, not knowing quite what to say. My mother handed me a package.

"This is from them. It is what you'll need to embrace this most important part of your life."

The new information answered questions about my past, but what did that mean regarding my future?

Opening the box, my hands searched beneath the tissue paper. At the bottom, there was a small beaded pouch. Loosening the drawstrings, I peered inside. There were only three small items, a shard of pottery with markings etched on it, a smooth piece of deerskin, and a photograph of my parents holding me as a newborn.

My parents … I carefully examined the picture trying to soak in every detail that it possessed.

My mother's figure was nothing like mine. She was very small-boned but tall. Her beautiful long black hair lay smoothed on the side of her face and held a flower in it She wore a pair of gold hoop earrings on her tiny ears. Her dress had a colorful pattern and fell gracefully off her shoulders. Her smile, as she gazed at the baby in her arms made me melt.

Father was taller. Even though he wasn't dressed in his traditional Navajo attire, the features of his ancestors were predominant. The bronzed complexion, high cheekbones, and a well-chiseled nose and forehead characterized these. His hair was black and long but pulled back in a ponytail. His smile was soft as if he were whispering to my mother or blowing kisses over me. The blanket enwrapping me was a handmade woven one, probably from one of my relatives.

"Ten minutes ago I was the archaeologist studying the people of this tribe, now I find myself to be a member of them?"

"I know this must be hard to digest dear. Are you upset with us from withholding this from you for so long?"

"No … I'm just not sure what I'm feeling right now."

"That's understandable. If you want to talk about it we're here for you, but if you'd rather be alone we'll respect that too."

"I just want to go to my room now if that's okay. I'll talk with you in the morning."

As I started to walk towards the door, my mother called to me.

"We both love you very much, Vickie."

"I know. I love you too. Goodnight."

The rest of that night was a blur. Before I knew it, the night was over and the sun was just coming up over the horizon. When I met my parents for breakfast, they could see I hadn't slept. I had so many questions, some of which they didn't have the answers too.

Would these "family" members even accept me? What about Evan? How could I just leave him and my career behind to pursue this quest for my relatives and piece together my "real" past?

They assured me they would be there to support me in any way they could. That afternoon, I left knowing that our relationship was as strong as ever.

The conflict within me grew, as the days passed, and I had not ventured to share my secret with anyone at the site. About a week and a half later, the excavation team turned its efforts to uncovering what seemed to be a burial site. A headstone didn't mark the grave, as usual, but there were other distinguishable features identifying it as such. The color of the grave fill was different from the soil around it.

As we carefully excavated, we found not only skeletal remains, but also traces of burial clothes and a few personal possessions. Pieces of pottery and stone stood out as grave offerings, while the animal bones found, henceforth indicated the last sacrificial meal. The deceased appeared to be a young woman with a stature of 5'1.

At first, my archaeological instincts took over, and I began helping. Then something struck me, the realization that this could have been one of my relatives, caused me to drop the trowel that I had been using, and stumble to the nearby tent. One of the other workers brought this to Evan's attention, as he had not witnessed my dramatic departure.

"Vickie, what's wrong? Are you alright," Evan asked, as he found me at the other end of the tent, hugging my knees.

"Yeah, I'll be okay. I....I never saw a real skeleton before. It just freaked me out that's all," I lied.

He laughed. "Is that all? Are you sure," he asked condescendingly as if I were a child.

Miffed that he'd taken it so lightly, I pulled myself up and headed for my cabin.

"Yes, everything's going to be alright," I retorted.

In my heart, I knew that wouldn't be the case, but I refused to let Evan sense what was going on inside my head.

During the time we had been excavating, there had been several bystanders on occasion. They never came close enough to get in the way, but the curiosity was there. Now that the pace was picking up, and the excitement growing, so was their interest. They seemed to be discussing the activities more, instead of just observing. We would soon find out the identity of those bystanders.

Ironically, not long after our burial discovery, the local Navajo tribe became actively interested. A confrontation soon reared its ugly head. Evan and Professor Perry were soon embroiled in a heated debate over sacred ground. If the tribe didn't receive the answer they wanted, they threatened to take care of the matter in other ways.

We left the area alone, in hopes that the confrontation would dissolve. After covering the grave, and moving the excavation to another location on the site, things seemed to be resolved.

Assuming this was the case; I let my guard down, and gave into investigating a cave in the canyon, after only two weeks without any stirrings. I wandered in, and thinking I was alone, concentrated not on my surroundings, but rather my exploration.

After hearing several muffled noises, the thought of coming face to face with a wild animal entered my thoughts. Alas, not soon enough, I began to realize the danger that lurked around the next corner. Anxiety set in, and gave way to panic, as I stumbled into the peril, which waited just beyond.

A strong arm came around from behind, went across my neck, and held onto my shoulder. He warned me not to scream, and walked me to an exit at the opposite end of the cave. Defenseless, I followed his order without a sound.

Our transportation awaited, an unsaddled horse, and as quickly as my assailant put me on it and sat behind me, we took off with lightning speed. There was a deafening sound of hoofs flying across the sand and over the gravel roads.

The heat emanated from his body. How I wished I had left my hair longer so as not to feel his breath against my bare neck. Although forceful, his silence remained for the entire ride. I kept a firm grip on my backpack, for it contained my past, present, and hopefully, my future.

After a long trek at a fast pace we slowed down, upon reaching the village. Hardly being able to stand, as I dismounted, he offered a strong arm for stability. Now, coming face-to-face with my alleged kidnapper, our stares became constant, neither flinching so as not to appear intimidated. Without a word, he led me to the committee of elders. Upset to see that this young man had taken matters personally, they apologized and assured me that this act was not acceptable, although neither were the actions at the excavation. They wanted to settle this matter as quickly as possible. Since I was already there, they asked me to act as a mediator between the two parties.

Rather than reveal my link to them at the outset, I waited. I wondered what would happen when Evan and the others realized that I was missing. Would Evan come and take me back? After the way I had avoided him since the discovery, I wouldn't blame him if he didn't. Maybe I didn't want him to. I was so confused, and my head was spinning wildly.

I was treated very well during the time spent waiting for Evan to be informed of the situation, and arrive at the meeting place. I decided to make the best of the predicament in which I found myself. After all, just because these people didn't know who I was, didn't mean I couldn't live alongside them, and learn from them. I used my anthropology skills to create a history, and began helping with chores.

The following day while working, I saw a coyote out of the corner of my eye. Normally I would have panicked, but after seeing how they interacted with these people, I learned not to cause undue alarm. Ignoring the animal, I went back to my assignment.

Within seconds, I heard a small child's scream. Looking up, I saw the coyote getting prepared to lunge at the girl. I screamed, ran toward her, and threw a piece of meat at the animal. It landed within a foot of the ravenous beast. It was enough of an enticement to divert it, and I grabbed the child from his sights. As he ripped apart the meal before him, I could see the white foam covering its mouth. Fortunately, for both of us, he took his prize and ran off into the woods.

It all happened so quickly, I didn't even realize I had the child in my arms. She was clinging to my neck and sobbing. Within seconds, Running Stag was beside us. We walked back to where everyone else had gathered.

Because of my bravery in saving Yazhi (Little One), a turquoise and silver necklace, that one of the young men in the tribe had made, was given for me to wear in remembrance of the day.

Lone Wolf was the one who had created the beautiful piece of jewelry called a squash blossom necklace. I watched this quiet one, wondering what he thought of my presence there. I had never seen a more beautiful human being. Tall, bronzed, and muscular, his beautiful long obsidian hair flowed freely. Around his head, there was a blood-red bandana, a white and gray feather hung from the knotted part. His dark eyes were close-set and showed intelligence and independence of spirit, yet they seemed to plead for friendship. His lips were full and his chin square. He had bands on both arms, along with a sleeveless shirt. There were beads strung around his neck. Watching him, I saw how his movements were swift and full of grace and virility.

Lone Wolf observed me from afar, and I sensed his curiosity. The flames blazed bright and cast shadows on his face, as he carved with an intense precision, the piece of flint he held in his fingers. The desire to speak with him was ever-present, but if he was a loner, as his name suggested, then he would have to be the one to make the first attempt, for him to feel at ease with my presence.

When he did speak to me for the first time, he whispered my name. I had not expected him to be so soft-spoken. I thought his voice would be loud and forceful, given his appearance.

Somewhere in our conversation, I felt compelled to stop hiding behind my veil of secrecy. He gave me all the reasons, trying to convince me why I belonged there.

"This is your family. You belong here. This is our way, our culture, and traditions, and it has brought us together."

He brought the matter to Wisdom of the Turtle, after asking my permission. Although, I think he would have told them anyway. Upon hearing the news, Wisdom of the Turtle had me brought before him right away.

I sat down, and cautiously handed Wisdom of the Turtle the only piece of my past I had given to me. He stared at the beaded pouch, and then began to examine it inside and out. It looked as if he were making sure of its authenticity.

He closed his eyes, and reached deep within himself, as he removed its contents and placed them before him. When he opened his eyes again, he picked up each item individually, first the remnant of deerskin, which he rubbed between his fingers, then the shard of pottery, finally the photograph. The tears welled up in his eyes.

"I cannot believe that you are here. For many years, we have wondered what had happened to your parents after they left here. We always hoped they would return to us."

"They both died of a respiratory disease when I was still a baby. I never knew them. My adopted parents brought me up. When I started becoming closer to the people of my real family, my mother told me about my heritage."

"She was wise to have given you this precious gift, your heritage, and I am glad of this," he smiled.

"I am very grateful that she did, but you will have to forgive me."

"What are we to forgive you for, my child?"

"Forgive me for not telling you this sooner. I wasn't sure if I wanted to come here or even if I was wanted here among you."

"But your heart tells you differently now."

"Yes, I know that I'm wanted here."

"Yes, we welcome you here with open arms and hearts. You must also consider your work. You have spent much time in schooling for this trade."

"I do want to be here among my family. I want to live and learn the ways. But …"

"Yes?"

"I've worked very hard in trying to reach my goals; and there are my family and friends also."

"This life will be a great challenge for you. Contact to let them know what has taken place will be necessary. The contact with them should be limited, at least at first so you may grow without distraction. Take the time to sleep on it before you make this important decision. Do not be hasty. There is much for you to consider. Naninago hazho' ogo adaa ahoninidzingo ninima."

He must have seen the puzzled look on my face because he translated for me.

"Walk in harmony within the universe by being aware of who you are."

"Thank you. I will."

A flute from which the sweet melodic sounds issued forth and wafted through the night air lulled me to sleep. The calming effect, a tranquil drum beat (like a heartbeat), and tingling bells harmoniously played together, became the native sound to which I was drawn. It opened a window to my past. I desperately wanted to know as much as I could about my heritage. How it would add to my personality and change my thinking and way of life was exciting to contemplate.

Evan came the next day, and I explained everything to him. My mediation served to bridge the gap between the two parties, but I needed to make a choice. Would I stay here or go back? It took me several days of walking alone to come to a reasonable decision.

Spending time with Lone Wolf would have only clouded my thoughts so he respectfully stayed away. He understood that the decision had to be mine, without outside influence. This way there would be no regrets or blame harbored afterward.

Finally, I made the difficult choice. Sadness loomed over the reservation, as I told them of my decision to go back.

Lone Wolf tried not to show his disappointment. Yet, his eyes gave away his thoughts. I now understood the saying, 'the eyes are the window into the soul.' The last memory I have of leaving that day was his demeanor. He stood tall with folded arms, and a look that tore away at my heart. He didn't even say or wave goodbye. He just stood there staring into a far off place. It was at that moment, I knew I had broken his heart. Something I never wanted to do.

We finished out the summer, and went back to classes in September. Evan and I continued seeing one another. Somehow, though, I couldn't get Lone Wolf or my family out of my mind. Although we never talked at length about it, I think Evan knew deep down inside that there was another force tugging at my heart, one that wanted to bring me home.

The following summer brought all the feelings flooding back, when we started a new excavation site not far from the old one. It affected my concentration, and left my work lacking any enjoyment.

While clearing out a new area for excavation my thoughts wandered. I wondered what my family was doing at that very moment. Would Lone Wolf want to see me? Not paying enough attention, coupled with leaning too much on my left leg, while it was in an awkward position, lead to the disaster. My leg buckled under me, with great pain from the applied stress. Falling to the ground with a hard thump, my first thought was that I had broken my leg. This was not the case. Instead, the predicament, which I found myself in, was a dislocated kneecap. The pain seared through me, I looked to see that my knee was almost behind my leg. I desperately needed to straighten my leg, so it would pop back into place, but I was too afraid to do it on my own.

I had the wind knocked out of me, so I couldn't call for help at first. Being in an isolated ditch, no one saw me fall. When my breath returned I yelled for assistance. Of course, as things weren't going right, Evan's absence for the day just compounded the situation.

Ann came to my rescue first and then went to get Charles and Professor Perry.

"If Evan were here he'd know what to do. His knee gives out all the time since that collision with the side of the mountain we went climbing. He all but completely shattered it."

I was extracted from the ditch and positioned so my leg could be straightened and the knee set right again. I prayed that it wouldn't pop out the other way, as I put a stick between my teeth and prepared for the worst.

The knee went back in, but a trip to the hospital was in order, when Evan returned. My leg was x-rayed, and fitted with a brace, which had my knee sticking through the hole in the middle of it. They added crutches to the ensemble before wheeling me out to the jeep for the long ride back.

The current state of affairs, which I found myself in, left me unable to perform certain tasks. Driving should have been one of them. Unfortunately, a rainstorm left a huge amount of mud in its wake. Since there were only three people in the van when it became stuck I had to "drive" with one good leg as the guys tried to push us out of the mire. It would have been funny at the time, had I not almost run them over while rocking the vehicle from drive to reverse in quick succession. In the process of trying to free ourselves, the fan belt fell out of the vehicle, and into the muck.

We felt bad for Charles, who left us in search of anyone who had a truck, and could come to our aid. In the meantime, Evan and I challenged each other to a game of wits, or as Aristotle termed it "educated insolence." The category was literature. The score to reach was twenty, in 2-point questions.

Evan selected the category; therefore, I asked the first perplexing question.

"What year did Arthur Miller win a Pulitzer Prize for Death of a Salesman (a. 1932, b. 1965, c. 1949, d. 1973)?"

"1949."

"Well, you're starting out on the right foot, your turn."

"Hmm, what novel started with the line, 'It is a truth universally acknowledged that a single man in possession of a good fortune must be in want of a wife.'?"

"Ah, you forgot that that novel is one of my favorites. That would be Pride and Prejudice."

"Very good."

"I'm not going to ask an easy one this time considering how fast you answered the last one."

"Fine, fine, give it your best shot."

"Okay, who said, 'Short words are best and the old words when short are best of all?'"

"Let's see. Would that be Sir Walter Scott?"

"No, it would not be, sorry. The answer is Winston Churchill."

"Humph. Try another one, please."

"What novel opened with the line, 'There was no possibility of taking a walk that day.'?"

"Jane Eyre."

"Right you are sir."

"Ah, I've got one for you. In the days when the spinning-wheels hummed busily in the farmhouses -- and even great ladies, clothed in silk and thread-lace, had their toy spinning-wheels of polished oak."

"It sounds familiar."

I placed my chin on my hand and thought hard. Then I repeated the question in an undertone.

"What was that? Did I hear a guess? You only get one per question you know," Evan said as he smiled mischievously.

"No, it wasn't a guess. I was merely repeating the question as I'm sure I know this one," I said with a British accent.

"Well if you know it, what is it? Come out with it," he prodded while mocking my accent.

"Would you just give me a moment to think please?"

Evan looked at his watch.

"Alright, you have exactly one minute starting now."

The time limit expired before I knew it, and I still hadn't come to any logical answer.

"Okay, I give up, what is it?"

"Silas Marner, by Mr. George Eliot himself," he sneered.

"And so it is. I knew I had read it before but I just couldn't place where. Well, we've each stumped one another once so far. Shall we continue?"

"I'm not going anywhere. Are you?"

We both laughed heartily at that one. Things seemed to be right between us once again. The game continued until I reached the 20-point mark. Feeling rather confident, after winning the first round, I challenged him to another. At the most inopportune time, the pain medication taken an hour before, dulled my brain cells. At least I'd like to think that was the reason for the defeat. In any event, he won by a landslide. We placed round three on the back burner, as Charles had returned with a Good Samaritan, and his truck.

After extraction from the mire, we reattached the fan belt, and got on the road, making our way back to the site. After dinner, and more medication, there was no way that, I could keep my eyes open, let alone play another rousing game of wits. My leg bothered me more that night, and I wished the two weeks of wearing the brace were finished.

I should have thanked the wonderful triage nurse in the emergency room. She made a "slight" mistake when she told me to keep the brace on for two weeks, instead of one. Because of this fact, my leg would not bend at all after we removed the brace. Rehabilitation was required. Finding a chiropractor wasn't an easy job either. When I did procure one, the exercises he had me carry out were excruciatingly painful.

Try to picture having to force yourself from lying on your stomach, to kneeling up on a leg that refuses to give at all. If that isn't enough to make you cringe, try adding the daily torture of leaning back further and further, in this position until it bends all the way. It was more painful than the actual dislocation itself. At least it was all set before the new semester started.

Another year of school finished, which brought me one year closer to "settling down" with Evan. He hadn't come out and asked me to marry him, but we did talk about it. I thought he was just waiting until I graduated. However, things didn't quite work out that way. Just before classes started up again, Evan received an offer to head a huge excavation in Scotland.

"Wow, that's a chance of a lifetime Evan. It's what you've been hoping for so long."

I tried to sound excited but I feared he heard the catch in my throat as I tried to hold back my tears.

"I haven't decided yet. I want to go but I want to be here with you too. I can't be in both places at once. The only thing I can think of is for you to join me in the summer instead of going to the field school."

"But it would almost be a year before I saw you again Evan."

"Well, maybe we can arrange for you to come out during the holiday and spring vacations too. We can e-mail and phone each other in between."

"Sure, I need to finish my studies anyway. It's too late now to apply to any universities in Scotland," I smiled.

"If you put in your application for the following year now, you'll be one step ahead of the game Vickie. I'll get all the information and paperwork you'll need once I'm settled, and send it to you. I am going to miss you dearly though," he whispered and kissed me on my head, nose, and then my lips.

"I'll miss you too Evan, more than you know."

Although I was trying desperately to believe that he loved me, he never reassured me with those words. Deep inside, I knew this was the end of our wonderful time together. At first, we e-mailed every day, sometimes two or three times. After things picked up with the excavation, it became two or three times a week. Since things didn't look too promising for a holiday visit, we planned for spring break.

Just before finals, Evan sent a letter by regular postal mail, telling me he wouldn't be in Scotland during my break from school. He had a conference to attend elsewhere to update everyone involved on the progress of the dig.

"Elsewhere, what does that mean? Why be vague as to where the conference was going to be held," I thought aloud.

Evan wrote once more after the conference to tell me how well it went. He sent his apologies about not being able to see me during that time but he never mentioned anything about the summer. When I didn't receive any more letters, I concluded that it was over. It was time to forget what we had and let go of him … forever.

That summer Ann, Charles, and I went to the field school for one last summer. It was like writing the final chapter to a novel that you thought would never end.

We all graduated the following June, and prepared to go in pursuit of our dreams. The promise of "we'll keep in touch" was foremost in our minds, and we were sincere about it. However, as we know from experience, life has a way of sliding in, and taking over. They were all good intentions. Would they be able to withstand the test of time though?

I truly had planned to pursue my goal of becoming a professional archaeologist. However, before I entered the graduate program, I wanted to visit Amber and Robert. Knowing that my intense studies could hinder me from traveling and visiting as much as I would like to for quite some time, I also went to "visit" the family that I had left behind, a visit that would be extended for quite some time.

From this point forward, I will be referring to the Navajo people as Dine' or The People. The word Navajo is Spanish for renegade, and is therefore undesirable. As you might have already guessed, my visit to the reservation turned into a decision to stay with my family. The sense of belonging held on tight this time, and was not about to let go without a fight. My new life began in the summer of 1982.

Hozjo means harmony, balance, and peace, and Dine' strive for in all aspects of a life, from the arrival at birth, clear through to the departure at death. Without it, one is not in touch with himself, much less the world around him.

I soon learned to which clans I belonged. When a Dine' baby is born, he or she belongs to the clan of the mother. The clan name passes on through her to her children. They are "born to" the mother's clan and take her clan name, and are "born for" the father's clan. Therefore, Dine' know precisely who they are, through identification by their mother's, father's, maternal and paternal grandfather's clans.

When a young man marries, it must be to someone completely outside of his clan. Even though people in his clan are not all blood-related, it is inappropriate to marry within one's clan. This rule must strictly be observed.

In my case, my mother was not a Dine' so this did not apply. My father's clan was the Dzi Ná'oodinii (Turning, Encircled Mountain People. My paternal grandfather's clan was the Haltsooí Dine'é (Meadow People).

Lone Wolf was born to the Ma'iitó (Coyote Spring People) and was born for the Yoo'í Dine'é (Bead People). His maternal grandfather's clan is the Dólii Dine'é (the Blue Bird People) and his paternal grandfather's clan is the Ma'iideeshgiizhinii (Coyote Pass People - Jemez Clan).

Lone Wolf forgave me for leaving the first time. He didn't waste any time in asking me to marry him, once he knew I was staying. Thankfully, our clans were not related to each other.

The Dine' weddings are simple yet elaborate ceremonies. They are simple, because not a lot of preparation is necessary for the location. Nature provides its flowers and beauty. They are elaborate, because of the importance placed on tradition.

Lone Wolf arranged to have several men play the love songs on flutes, drums, rattles, and whistles. We invited everyone from both extended families, along with the community to celebrate the marriage. Of course, I invited my adoptive parents. Wisdom of the Turtle was the officiating elder.

Since I was new to all of this, I needed help in preparing decorative willow baskets to hold the gifts. We also designed and made our wedding attire. The wedding basket or Ts'aa' was woven, made entirely out of sumac, and decorated with natural dyes. This basket compared to a map through which we chart our lives. White cornmeal symbolizes the male and yellow cornmeal, the female. We combined the two meals into a corn mush and put it into a wedding basket before the traditional ceremony. At a Dine' marriage, a new basket is required to serve traditional cornmeal mush to the wedding couple, and then it is passed around for the guests.

We made gifts for Wisdom of the Turtle and our mothers.

A week before we were married, Lone Wolf's parents made the Wedding Vase. Then they, along with my parents, and all his relatives came to my house. I brought out everything I needed to establish our new home together: clothing, utensils, mattress, moccasins, corn, and some other homemaking items. I was especially proud of my white manta wedding dress that I helped to make. Lone Wolf took one look at the dress and exclaimed, "Nizhoni (It's beautiful)."

Our parents gave us advice to help us have a happy and successful marriage. They placed the water in the Wedding Vase. They turned it around, and handed it to me first. I drank from one side of it, turned it around again, and gave it to Lone Wolf, who then drank from the opposite side of it. This united us as one.

The day finally came. Both friends and family brought food for the wedding feast.

Our wedding rings were made of sterling silver with turquoise inlay all the way around in the shape of triangles. My ring had the turquoise inlaid in one direction and onyx in the opposite direction. As we exchanged them, Wisdom of the Turtle spoke.

"The marking of the passage to the status of husband and wife is marked by the exchange of rings. These rings are a symbol of the unbroken circle of love. Love, freely given, has no beginning and no end, no one giver and no one receiver, for each is the giver and each is a receiver. Let these rings always remind you of the vows you make to each other today."

He bestowed upon us the most beautiful wedding blessing, which I will never forget.

"Now you will feel no rain, for each of you will be a shelter for the other. Now you will feel no cold, for each of you will be warmth for the other. Now you are two persons, but there is only one life before you. Go now to your dwelling, to enter into the days of your life together. And may your days be good and long upon the earth."

Looking deeply into each other's eyes, we kissed. As his arms wrapped around me, I knew I was where I should have been all along. Everyone and everything around us disappeared, and we were the only two people left on this earth, until the music and festivities started.

There was singing, along with instrumental music. The men formed a group, and sat around a large double-headed drum, singing in unison and drumming with sticks. Everything was so wonderful. I felt the tears welling up. Lone Wolf saw the joy in my eyes, and gave me a heartwarming smile. We had found our soul mates in each other.

We felt very blessed to welcome twins, a girl, and a boy, only ten months after we were married. I was determined to have them grow up with as much of their culture and language as possible. I wanted them to experience their heritage from the very beginning of their life.

They both were strong and strong-willed. Our son showed signs of this from the very start. He was only a few days old when he was able to hold his head up, on his own. Because of this fact, we named him Bidziil, meaning he is strong. We found this to be true when he cried too. He had a good set of lungs to be sure.

Our daughter was very attentive to everyone around her. Smiles emanated from her almost all the time. Therefore, we named her Doli, meaning bluebird. Even the animals drew close to her. She gave a peaceful calming effect to anyone who held her.

Watching them grow and learn, gave us such joy. They picked up and understood both languages faster than I could understand the Dine' language. There were hundreds of questions, which all seemed to begin with the word "why."

As twins, they played and explored together, they always watched out for each another. Even though they were born only a half-hour apart Bidziil protected Doli as if he were years older. It was funny at night to hear them whisper to each other, thinking we couldn't hear. It was hard not to laugh at some of the ways they looked at things.

Lone Wolf made a wonderful father. He was loving and kind, but stern. He melted at his daughter's smile, but refrained from giving in to her every whim, he refused to let her wrap him around her little finger. Well, at least he thought he did, so I let him believe it. He taught his son all the things he needed to know about tool making and hunting. Bidziil learned quickly and became very adept at both skills. Together they build our new home and we moved from the Hogan soon after.

One night after the children had fallen asleep, Lone Wolf turned to me. He looked deep into my eyes.

"Sahkyo (Mink), you have made me the happiest man on this earth. Your love for our children and me warms my heart. Your beauty shines and your face shows your happiness. I don't know what I would have done if you hadn't come back to me. You have made me the man I am today."

The tears streaming down my cheeks accompanied my smile. Deep inside was a feeling I had never experienced before. The love we shared was true, faithful, and timeless. Our love encompassed our minds and bodies. We gave everything to each other and our two beautiful children. We wanted nothing else in this world but to see them mature, and make lives of their own, while we grew old together.

That dream seemed to be shatter into tiny pieces, when I became severely ill one winter's night. I awakened not only myself, but also my entire family, with a scream that came from deep within me. Lone Wolf jumped up, only to find me bleeding profusely.

He had Doli stay with me, while he raced to the shaman's (medicine man) Hogan.

At only ten, my poor daughter was frightened out of her mind, when she first came to my bedside.

Lone Wolf instructed Bidziil to stand guard outside the room, but not to enter. With all the courage he could muster, he stood straight and tall at his post, never wavering, until his father's return.

I was already unconscious when they arrived. After a quick and decided examination, the shaman concluded that I had lost our third child. His instructions needed following to the letter, if I was to have any chance at survival. Given the circumstances, he didn't give much hope of that, even if they were.

For nine days, the fever held on, as I went in and out of consciousness. Lone Wolf stayed by my side constantly. The children busied themselves with chores, while they comforted each other. Finally, on the tenth day, the fever broke, and I regained consciousness. My thoughts and memories of those days were forever lost.

Those days made the children grown up a little faster. They became more responsible and understanding, as the effects of the fever lingered on for some months afterward.

Lone Wolf became different, after my brush with death. In his eyes, you could see that he had lost a part of himself, as did I. The torment of losing our child, and almost losing me, left him overwhelmed. Waking up to his sobbing one night, I wrapped myself in our blanket, and followed the sound into the living room. There he sat, with his head in his hands. It was hard to see him in the dark, but hearing him, brought my heart to my throat, and tears to my eyes. He was proud, but not too proud to show his feelings. This made my love and respect for him even stronger.

"I'm sorry Sahkyo; I didn't mean to wake you. Sleep escapes me tonight. So many thoughts are running through my mind."

Taking me in his arms and drawing me closer, I felt the tears upon his face and wiped them with my hair. He whispered so softly that his breath washed over me.

"I love you Sahkyo and I never want to lose you. When I think how ..."

He shuddered as he drew in a sharp breath.

"But you didn't lose me. I'm here with you. See?"

Putting his face in my hands, I brought it closer to mine, and kissed him. He responded slowly and thoughtfully at first, but then, all the feelings built up inside burst forth. His lips recaptured mine and covered over them with a burning intensity. He gave up every part of his being to me, and took mine in return. Exhausted and content we fell asleep within each other's embrace.

Children see things much differently than adults. They don't see barriers, unless instilled within them by older ones. Looking through the eyes of a child, we can begin with the simplest of human behavior, play. In comparing my childhood to that of my children, I saw both differences and similarities. Some of the games were versions of ones that I had enjoyed as a child.

Take for instance the game of Solemnity. The idea is to have one member challenge another to a test of ability, to keep one's "face straight." Facing each other, and in the presence of the crowd, each looks into the other's eyes to see which will smile or laugh first. If desired, add speech and gestures to the rules. We called this "make me laugh." There was even a television show by that name when I was growing up.

Then there is the Game of Menagerie. The players sit in a circle. One begins, "As I went to the Menagerie..." His neighbor to the right asks, "What did you see there?" He answers, "I saw a lion." The neighbor then turns to his right-hand neighbor and says, "I went to the Menagerie." Ask the same question, "What did you see there?" The second player must then repeat the answer of the first, "I saw a lion," adding to it an animal of his own, "and a monkey." The game goes on in this way, each player putting the same question and answer of his neighbor and adding the name of another animal. Is this game sounding familiar to anyone?

There was the rendition of arm wrestling termed Strong Hand or Hand Wrestling. It was a little different in the fact that we used to sit for this game. Here, the two contestants stand right foot by right foot, right hands clasped together; left feet braced; left hands behind. At the word "go," each tries to unbalance the other; that is, make him lift or move one of his feet. A lift or a shift ends the round.

Watching them play these games like these, and others that I came to learn through them, was all part of the joy I experienced in reliving my childhood in a native light. We used games for teaching too. To help the children learn geography we played this game at the dinner table. The first player begins by naming a geographical place, such as a mountain, river, city, state, or nation; the next player gives another name, which must be geographical and the first letter of which must be the same as the last letter of the name given by the first player. For instance, the first player names Alabama; the second player names Arkansas, the third player names Saskatchewan, the fourth player the Nile. It helped them tremendously. So much so, that Doli won the geography bee at school in sixth grade.

Bidziil was academically smart as well, but he took more pride in his athletic skills. He adored archery and track and field. His marksmanship was precise. While running like lightning, he often left his teammates trailing behind in his dust.

My parents came to share in the accomplishments of their grandchildren several times during the year. I was so happy to have them be a part of their lives, along with Lone Wolf's parents. They would grow to be well-rounded individuals, with a history from two cultures. Doli learned to weave from her nali (grandmother) and gave what she made to her grandma. Bidziil learned to play chess from his grandpa. He spent time learning the Dine' ways from his nálí (grandfather) as well. They truly felt special to have a set of grandparents from each culture.

As the years passed, we made and maintained strong relationships. It was difficult at first, for Lone Wolf to leave the reservation and travel to my parents' house. Because he had spent his entire life on the reservation, it did not sit well to request that our children do any different. He felt that they might one day leave the reservation for good, if they thought there was something better outside of it. Without ever saying it, I knew he had my birth parents in mind when the matter arose.

When we did leave the reservation for visits though, he became like a child in some ways himself. His eyes would light up when he became fascinated with the things he had never seen before. The city and its faced paced ways were in stark contrast to the slower life he had come to know and love. Although he chose that which he held dear to his heart, he came to appreciate how those trips meant so much to me. After my parents died, he and I were glad that we had taken the opportunity to spend the time we had with them.

As the children grew and learned new things, the elements of my heritage became clear, and added to the person I had become. Missing some parts of it earlier in life, I found happiness and peace, in the years spent piecing my life together.

Two of our life's essentials were water and wood. The juniper and pine trees served us well in this regard. The men cut the trees into logs, then stacked and let them dried. This was crucial when it came time to use the supply to warm our homes and ourselves. We also used them to cook our meals.

Learning to make a Be'e'zo' or a grass brush was something I taught Doli. We used yucca root to make shampoo. We used the leaves to tie and hold together the dried perennial grass, which made the brush. It made a light scratching sound as I brushed Doli's clean shiny hair. She had the same long dark obsidian hair as her father.

Some of the crafts learned, took me back to my archaeology days. It happened once, when we were at the clay pits getting what we needed to make new pottery. We used the shovel to loosen and break up the hard chunks of clay. As soon as I began, my thoughts brought me back to the day we started preparing the site for excavation. They wandered so far away from my task, that I must have stopped digging. In the distance, I heard (my mother-in-law) call my name, and I snapped out of my trance.

"Are you well, Sahkyo?"

"Of course, I was just thinking of something and it sidetracked me."

"They are thoughts of days long ago?"

"Yes. How did you know that?"

"I have watched you for a long time my daughter. There are times when I see in your eyes the life you used to know. Do you miss it terribly?"

"No, not terribly, there are just some things that I do which remind me of them."

"Sometimes it worries me to see that look in your eyes. I begin to wonder if you regret coming here and leaving all those things behind."

"Never, I could no sooner leave and go back to that life than to cut off my right arm. My place is here with my family. I have Lone Wolf and my children. What more could I ask for in life?"

"I'm glad to hear you say that Sahkyo. You have made my son very happy over the years. My heart was worried about him at one time. When you left the first time, he walked around with a crushed spirit for many days. When you returned, I was not sure that having you in our family was the best thing. But I see now that it was the right and best decision he could have ever made."

"Thank you, Ooljee (Moon). Hearing you say that means a great deal to me. I don't know what I would do if I didn't have Lone Wolf in my life."

As a tear fell on her cheek, she looked at the ground. Composing herself she said, "Well if we are going to be making any pottery, we need to finish getting the clay. We still have to go into the forest to collect the pitch from the pinion (pine) trees. That is what we will use for the glaze to seal the pot when it is finished."

We finished with the clay and the pitch, before we continued in search of the other needed items. Collecting cinder stone, which, when ground, would become red lava cinders, and firewood would be accomplished too before we could even begin. As we swept the fine red powder onto the screen, which we used as a sieve, another flashback occurred. The distant look in my eyes went unnoticed this time though.

Hunting was something essential to provide for the people of the tribe. Along with this, came the ceremony associated with a sweat lodge. This would purge the body of any human odors, detected by a wary deer.

Being only for the men, I did not see the lodge myself, but Lone Wolf told me of the experience.

"The sweat lodge resembles a giant beehive. A fire burns a few feet away, to prepare the rocks for the ceremony. We heated them until they were glowing red. They were then put inside the lodge in the northern corner."

"Why the northern corner," I asked forgetting my manners and interrupting.

Lone Wolf was kind, and understood my curiosity. He laughed then continued with his story.

"This wards off any north wind. Then we removed any clothing and crawled into the lodge. We dropped the blanket door, and instantly, we felt the heat, which was hot enough to bake our skin. The sweat was just streaming from me. Then there was a loud crack, as Running Bear poured water mixed with pine needles and cedar on the hot glowing red rocks."

My eyes opened wide as I saw the excitement in his, as he described what happened next.

"Suddenly there was an unbearable rush of hot vapor emanating from the rocks. It was overpowering. It vanished just as quickly as it came. The smell of burning needles calmed me. He did this several times. We sipped the mixture, handed to us. It felt good, as it cleansed me here," he said as he took my hand and ran it from his throat to his abdomen.

A chill ran down my spine as he went on with the story.

"We crawled out, dripping into the cold air, which made us shiver a little. Then we rolled around in the sand."

"You did what," I interrupted again.

"Yes, it is like a coarse soap, ridding us of any dead skin. Then we go back into the lodge and do everything a second time. After this, we dress and get prepared to leave for the hunt. Now, what do you think of that Sahkyo," he teased.

"I find it very interesting."

"I thought you would."

His eyes grew wide as he drew me to him. Even after years of being together the desire never waned. Just the brush of his hand across my face sent, thousands of electrical charges through me. His deep gaze searched my eyes, as he felt my body tremble under his touch.

"Just looking at you Sahkyo makes my heart leap," he whispered.

Placing my arms around his neck, I loosened his hair, and whispered, "My wonderful man."

With one fluid movement, he lifted me off my feet, and into the cradle of his strong loving arms. Contented, I rested against the warm lines of his body, as he carried me to our room.

We woke early the next morning though not getting much sleep the night before. Getting ready, and heading out to the annual fair, was the day's project. I think we were as excited about going as the children. Looking forward to seeing all our relatives, sharing in the festivities, and sampling different variations of traditional foods were just some of the reasons we were eager to get there.

There was much to see on the way. One of my favorite landscapes has always been the weathered rock formations at the edge of Todicheenie Bench, northwest of Kayenta. They look like someone used a giant pottery wheel to create them. Instead of molding the clay as it spun around, it stayed in the rippling stage. For those familiar with the top shell of a clam or quahog, the formations on the very top are exaggerated versions of these in both shape and texture. Adding to this is the beauty of the Monument Valley monoliths seen in the far horizon, connecting the two as one reservation.

The beauty of the painted landscapes was awe-inspiring. The majestic mountains, weathered red monoliths, pure white sand coupled with crystal waters and tall green trees all make up Dintah, our "promised land."

The Four Corners, or the eighth wonder of the world, is the four-state intersection of Arizona, Colorado, New Mexico, and Utah. This is the land of the Dine', the place we call home. History tells us the story of "how the west was won," but for us, it was a time of "how the west was lost." It took many years for our ancestors to reclaim some of the land given to our people. Even then, it was with animosity that they handed it over. We cherish the land, respect, and work in harmony with it.

So many happy times filled the next few years together. It solidified our love and desire to be as one forever.

The day we gave our daughter in marriage to Naalnish (he who works), was something out of a fairy tale. Watching the look in their eyes, and seeing the true love they had for one another, brought me back to the day Lone Wolf and I became man and wife.

Yet, torn from us only nine months later, was our family's happiness, leaving us not only scarred but gaping holes within us, for the rest of our lives.

The reservation police officers arrived at the door at the time I expected the men to be home. Seeing the look on the officers' faces when I opened the door told me something was very wrong.

While they told me of the accident, I became weak and fell to my knees by the couch. There was no comfort in the world, which could've helped me then. Though the officers tried their best, they had torn hearts too, as they could only imagine the pain I was feeling.

I don't even remember going with them to the hospital. I do remember crying out in pain as the doctor's words seared through my mind and heart.

Bidziil never knew what happened, as he slept in the passenger seat. Lone Wolf was still alive when the ambulance arrived, but his injuries had been too severe for them to save him. He had expired before they reached the hospital. Lone Wolf's driving drifted, until they veered off the road and crashed into a tree.

While trying to digest the horrible news, I turned to hear Doli coming to me from down the hall. She and Naalnish seemed to be running in slow motion. Doli's arms flung around me, and held me tight, as we sobbed on each other. The doctor led the three of us into the family room, where we could be alone to grieve.

As the years past, I found myself not forgetting Lone Wolf and Bidziil, but the memories became blurred. Although Doli, Naalnish, and their children have kept their love alive, traveling back and forth from the reservation to my home in Colorado, bringing back beautiful treasures each time.

The last thing I wanted was to come to the place where it all became a dream and not reality. Thus, the reasons why I penned the words in this book emerged. It wasn't as easy to do, as one might think. Yes, the memories and experiences relived seemed as if they had just happened, but these brought with it a flood of emotions. These periods of emotional instability drained me to the point of having to stop my writing several times, before being able to complete them all as a manuscript.

After publication, I decided to promote my story with book signings around the country. Starting from the East and working my way back home, became the plan, making it full circle. The last signing I did was in a little book store outside Phoenix. It was a great success. The two hours flew by while I signed an endless amount of books, and conversed with people who were truly interested in my work. As I raised my eyes, to acknowledge the last person in line, I was stunned. Before me, stood a man whom I had not seen in over two decades.

"Hello Vickie," he said with a smile.

## Epilogue

I will never forget Lone Wolf, as the beautiful memory of his love lives within me. My family assured me that although they didn't want me to leave; I was always welcome to come home again. I have visited on many occasions, but another passion fills my time now - my life as a professional archaeologist, author, and the wife of Dr. Evan Carter.

In essence, I have lived two lifetimes in one, shared the love of two families, two men, and two passions. I could never have asked for anything more, as my life has more happiness than I could have ever imagined.

I give my love and thankfulness to Stephen and Madeline Singer, and all those in my extended Dine' family; they have truly helped me become the woman I am today.

To my sweet son Bidziil, your memory is deep within my heart.

To my daughter Doli, son-in-law Naalnish, and my grandchildren, thank you for your love and support throughout the years.

If I leave nothing else in this world when I depart, please remember that I left my thumbprints in the stream of time. – Mrs. Victoria Carter PHD

Ha go ney. (Walk in beauty.)

Printed in Great Britain
by Amazon